Royal Tiger

Zoe Chant

Also by Zoe Chant

Shifter Kingdom

Royal Guard Lion

Fire & Rescue Shifters

Firefighter Dragon

Firefighter Pegasus

Firefighter Griffin

1

TRISTAN

Tristan had been a member of the Royal Guard for ten years. He had served on the king's personal guard detail for most of that time. He had seen the king asleep and awake, in anger and joy, and in a grief that came dangerously close to madness.

Like every guardsman, he had come perilously close to failing in his duty to protect the king in the last several months. Princess Signy, newly come to the kingdom from America, where she had grown up unknowing her Valtyran heritage and royal status, had been the key to foiling the First Minister's cowardly plot against the king. None of the guardsmen had seen it, or understood what they were seeing, until it was nearly too late.

Tristan was the only one summoned to an audience with the king after the official ceremony recognizing the new Crown Prince and Crown Princess.

All had come right, it seemed. The princess was

betrothed, and her mate, Kai, was to rule the kingdom by her side when the king finally passed from the throne. The villains had been routed—the scheming First Minister, Otto, had fled with his nephew Nikolai, and the traitorous guardsman Peter was under lock and key. Tristan had been the one to secure him while Kai got Princess Signy to safety; the cut he had taken from Peter's dragon claws no longer required a bandage, thought it had left scars across his cheek and the side of his throat.

By all rights, Tristan was a hero, nearly as much as the new Prince Kai. He should have nothing to fear of a private audience with the king he had served so long and so faithfully. Kai had been a friend of Tristan's for years, and Princess Signy seemed to like him well enough. Only a few hours earlier, while he stood as a ceremonial guard over the luncheon celebrating Kai's investiture as Crown Prince, she had cast him smiling looks.

Still, under the cool, expressionless mask he had cultivated long before he entered the Royal Guard, Tristan could not help fearing that some punishment was about to fall upon him.

Well, if it was, he would stand and take it. He was the king's man, and had renounced all other ties to serve the king as a member of the Royal Guard. If the king saw fit to punish him—and surely, if he were to be rewarded, it would be a public affair—he would accept the will of the king.

Tristan was taken aback when he stepped through the door of the king's private office and discovered that he was, in fact, far from being alone with the king. Not only were Princess Signy and Prince Kai in attendance, but also Princess Signy's mother and stepfather—Mary and Frank Zlotsky, since Princess Mary had declined to retain the title she had from marrying Princess Signy's father, Prince Alexander, who had died twenty-three years ago.

Tristan bowed, feeling a confusion that he knew his face and posture would not betray to those around him.

2

"Your Majesty. Have I mistaken the time?"

"Not at all, Tristan," the king assured him. "I thought it simplest to assemble everyone most closely concerned with the mission I am to assign you, at my granddaughter's request."

Tristan looked at Princess Signy, who was giving him the same smiling, thoughtful look he had seen on her face that morning. Tristan—along with Kai, who had been his brother guardsman until just days ago—had been sent out on a special mission by the king only a couple of weeks earlier. They had gone to America, to find Princess Signy and to guard her until her return to Valtyra.

Perhaps he was only to go and retrieve some things for Princess Signy? Or escort her parents somewhere? Though he had thought they intended to stay in Valtyra until the royal wedding, which was scheduled for just a few days from now.

"I serve according to Your Majesty's pleasure," Tristan assented quietly, with another small bow.

"It's my little sister," Princess Signy explained when Tristan had straightened up.

She glanced toward her mother and the stepfather who had raised her since she was a toddler, and clarified, "Half-sister, of course. Poppy Zlotsky is her full name—she just turned twenty-one a couple of weeks ago, and I haven't seen her in nearly a year. She's been backpacking, hitchhiking, just... wandering, I suppose. She let us know a few days ago that we might not be able to reach her for a while, and now we can't find her or get in touch with her. She knows how to look out for herself, obviously, but..."

Princess Signy's voice faltered away to nothing, and she looked over to Prince Kai, who gripped her hand firmly in his.

"Otto and Nikolai are obviously a danger," Kai said briskly, as he would have spoken to Tristan when they were both still guardsmen, assessing some threat. "If they try to get hold of her for leverage, or mess with her head the way they did with Peter's..."

Tristan allowed his face to show a faint wince, a tightening around his eyes and upper lip. He felt his new scars pull a little as he did.

Peter insisted—truthfully, as far as anyone could discern—that his treason had been well-intended. Otto and Nikolai had convinced Peter that it was Princess Signy who plotted against the king, and that she must be stopped by any means necessary, before she was able to consolidate her power. Peter had believed, when he saw Kai break ranks with the other guardsmen to dance with the princess, that she would soon use Kai to strike against the king, and so had attacked first.

Tristan could imagine what Otto might make of Princess Signy's younger sister—she was obviously resourceful, to have made her way alone in the world for so long as a young woman. If Otto persuaded her that Signy had been kidnapped away to Valtyra, held prisoner under some wicked enthrallment, and only her sister could free her...

"I see," Tristan said. "Of course."

Kai nodded. "Hopefully he'll have at least as much trouble finding her as we will. And he might overlook her entirely, since she's..."

Kai looked apologetically toward Princess Signy and the Zlotskys before he finished, "Human."

Princess Signy was human herself, of course, or she would not need a mate to rule the kingdom of shifters after her grandfather. Her father, Prince Alexander, had been a bear shifter like the king.

Many shifters thought that of humans as less than shifters—particularly those of a more conservative type, the *Valtyra is for Valtyrans* kind, who meant by it, *Valtyra is for shifters*. Never mind that even in the most ancient shifter families human children were born in practically every generation. Never mind that those humans were every bit as Valtyran as their brothers and sisters, or that there were certain ancient strains of magic, vital to the kingdom, that only humans could perform. Valtyra was ruled by shifters, and in the eyes of some shifters that would always mean that humans were something other, something less.

Tristan had been familiar all his life with that kind of thinking. He had rejected it along with his family's name when he entered the Royal Guard. He had had to, because even ten years ago, when Princess Signy had never set foot in Valtyra, it had been well known that the royal family included a human princess. She had been foreign-born and as good as lost to them, but nonetheless it was known that she would be protected by the Royal Guard if they ever found her.

Tristan nodded now to Kai. "A weakness we may benefit from, if our enemy underestimates Miss Zlotsky."

Kai smiled, a bright, open expression that suited the lion prince, and nodded back. "Yes, indeed."

"So we come to your mission," the king put in.

Tristan focused on him, snapping to attention.

"You are to locate Miss Zlotsky by any ordinary or magical means that may serve. No expense is to be spared. If you must call on foreign assistance, you shall have my backing. If you require support from your brother guardsmen, requisition them as you need. You shall have command of any you select to bring into Miss Zlotsky's guard detail. Though she is not royal in herself, yet she is family to the Crown Princess—much loved, and to be protected the same, by my order as king."

Tristan bowed more deeply than he had yet. "As Your Majesty wills."

He was already thinking of a dozen avenues of inquiry—he would have to get as thorough a history as Princess Signy and the Zlotskys could provide of Miss Zlotsky's movements, and any particular friends or associates, any more distant family she might call upon or favorite places she might visit...

"And we're pushing the wedding back a little," Princess

Signy added, snapping Tristan out of his thoughts.

Kai groaned—not real protest, but a show of frustration, as he sat there with his arm around his mate. Tristan knew very well that they were not in *that* much suspense for the wedding night. He had, briefly, shared a hotel suite with them in America, after they recognized each other as mates.

Very briefly. The lobby had been extremely well-patrolled that night, and Tristan had had plenty of time to reflect on a decade of nearly total celibacy. While guardsmen were not required to forego sex entirely, Tristan had never gotten the knack of taking it lightly. A serious relationship would mean the end of his service, and while Tristan supposed it was still possible that his mate might turn up somewhere, nothing less was worth it to him.

Nor, in honesty, did he expect that someone as reserved and remote as himself would be worth the trouble to anyone who did not recognize *him* as her mate. He did not have Kai's bright, cheerful charm; he did not even stumble over himself and blush the way many of the younger guardsmen would, in the presence of an attractive woman. He was simply stone, as immovable as the mountains, and had been for a very long time. He wasn't sure he would know how to be anything else even if he did meet his mate.

Still, watching his best friend's bliss made him wonder what it would be like if he had the chance to try.

"I'd really like Poppy to be there," Princess Signy went on, quite unaware of Tristan's thoughts. "But Lady Teresa says if I put it back more than two weeks it will throw off the entire social calendar and she'll make us wait until next year. So I understand if it's not possible to find her in time, of course, but... you'll try, won't you?"

The princess gave him a dazzling, hopeful smile, and Tristan glanced from Kai to the king and thought that he might have been right the first time. He was being punished.

"I'll do everything in my power, Your Highness," he said, letting none of his trepidation show.

"And you can't force her to come back," Mrs. Zlotsky said, speaking up for the first time. "She won't listen, you know, and she'll hate it. You have to convince her to come—make her think it's her own idea, if you can."

"But don't tell her *everything*," Princess Signy added. "I mean—I'd like to explain some of it to her myself, you know? About Valtyra, and being a princess, and everything."

"But you can't lie to her," Mrs. Zlotsky put in, and her husband and Princess Signy both nodded quick agreement to that.

Tristan nodded along with them. He was definitely being punished.

~~*

Tristan was briefly hopeful that magic would be of some help, at least in *finding* Miss Zlotsky, if not in persuading her to come back to Valtyra without lying to her or revealing too many secrets or being too forceful or too slow. But all the best practitioners, when summoned to the palace to make the attempt, could only determine that Miss Zlotsky was not anywhere in Valtyra, and probably not in Denmark.

A search conducted with the help of the nearest sea dragons to the coast, which required Tristan to stand ankle-deep in the surf as the moon rose, concluded that she was certainly not in or under the North Sea, and probably not in any closely connected waterway.

"Though you know how it is these days, with the iron boats," the sea dragon woman said. She stood half a head taller than Tristan. Her brown skin, several shades darker than his, was perfectly smooth, but her vivid blue hair had faded to a silvery paleness. She might well remember when iron boats were a far rarer presence in these waters. "She might not be so very far away."

Tristan accepted that half-hopeful pronouncement as the best he was likely to get. He reported to Princess Signy and her parents that night only the better part of what all the searchers had agreed upon: Poppy was alive, and likely not more than two or three thousand miles away at most, and probably not in very great danger at the moment.

"It's easier to find them then," a witch of the sparrowhawk clan had explained to him. "When they're crying out to be found—especially when you're searching through a family tie."

The woman had gestured to the locks of hair and drops of blood Princess Signy and her parents had contributed.

Tristan couldn't help thinking that his own family were the last people he would wish to be found by, if he had gotten into any kind of trouble in the last ten years. He would call out for help to his brother guardsmen, maybe, or simply do everything he could to survive, to keep control of himself and do his duty.

All he had wanted from his family, for a very long time before he left, was to escape them.

He had a hard time imagining that anyone would feel the same about Princess Signy and the Zlotskys—but then his own parents had not been cruel. Not as they understood it. They had simply thought that they knew Tristan better than he knew himself, and that they knew what was best for him.

If the Royal Guard had not been the most obvious way to escape—if he had not been a shifter, wary of the human world even though he knew his wariness was mostly an echo of his family's prejudice—would he have done what Poppy Zlotsky did, and fled to wander the world? He had been just about the age she was now when he finally left his family for the Royal Guard.

Would he have learned to be different then? To show himself more, to loosen the tight control? Or would he have become only more rigid, alone in a world of strangers?

But those questions were irrelevant, surely. Whatever he might have become in similar circumstances, he had no special kinship with Poppy Zlotsky. He had merely been assigned to find her. There was no reason to think that he understood her better than her own family did.

That was going to make it difficult to locate her when they could not, never mind somehow persuading her to return to Valtyra when he knew himself to have all the charm and allure of a cliff face, but Tristan had his mission. He would find some way to complete it.

$*\sim*\sim*$

Tristan spent hours studying the photographs Poppy Zlotsky had taken over the last year—most of them on her public Instagram account, and others, carefully noted and placed in the correct sequence, that she had sent privately to her mother, father, or sister.

Poppy herself appeared in a fair number of the pictures; there were selfies taken at arm's or stick's length, and others, usually group shots, where Poppy must have handed over her camera to a friend or perhaps a stranger.

Seeing her cheerful, sweet smile again and again, Tristan had no trouble believing that she would be able to charm anyone she met into doing her such a service. He was also more sure than ever that he and Poppy had nothing at all in common.

Tristan tried not to see her beauty as anything other than a useful piece of information about the woman he was seeking. She was petite like her mother, short and slim with hair of a brilliant copper color that caught the light in one picture after another. Her eyes were a curious mixed hazel color, looking sometimes gray, sometimes strikingly green. She had freckles sometimes, if she had been out in the sun a good deal, dappling her pale skin. Her arms and legs, frequently revealed by sleeveless shirts and rather scanty shorts, hinted at considerable strength in her small frame—as did the many references to hiking and climbing in various forbidding places.

It would indeed be a mistake to underestimate Poppy Zlotsky.

There were a variety of other people in Poppy's photos, but only a handful who showed up more than once or twice, and Tristan couldn't track down anything like full names or proper contact information for any of them. He mapped her route over the last year as best he could, but many of the locations were unspecified, and some of the ones that were conflicted with the itineraries Princess Signy and the Zlotskys had written out with their best guesses of Poppy's location over the last year.

Tristan sat back in his chair and rubbed at his eyes, burning from staring intently at the fine details in one picture after another, scrolling through endless badly-punctuated comments on photos in search of clues about location or the identities of Poppy's... friends? Acquaintances? Traveling companions?

He needed help with this. He had been told he could requisition any guardsmen he needed, but the Royal Guard was stretched thin already. They had more people to guard, with the new additions to the royal family, and fewer men to do it with thanks to the losses of Kai, Peter, and Nikolai from their ranks, as well as Tristan himself.

And that was to say nothing of the unpleasant suspicion that lingered around several of the guards. It was impossible to know who might have had a word dropped in his ear by the First Minister, or turned a blind eye to the way the king got sicker and sicker after the previous Crown Prince's death. Could Tristan ask any of them to help him find Poppy, and be sure he wouldn't feed the information directly to Otto instead?

All the men he knew best from years of serving by their sides were exactly the ones he couldn't bring himself to take off the guard rotations. The younger ones—who were probably better at figuring out all this internet stuff, and might know enough of human ways to be helpful in finding Poppy—were exactly the ones he couldn't help suspecting.

Something made him think of Peter, then. He had personally locked up the young guardsman—who was just Poppy Zlotsky's age, in fact—on the night of his attack against Princess Signy. Tristan had stayed there, guarding the cell, until the Captain of the Guard and the king came down to get Peter's story, and Tristan had waited just outside and listened to Peter's tearful confession, his pleas for forgiveness.

I never meant to put you in danger, sir, Peter had pleaded. *I only meant to help. If there's anything I can do to prove it, I will.*

Peter was still being held in a cell until the king had time to decide just what to do with him in the long run. His Majesty was inclined to be merciful, Tristan knew, and Princess Signy was rather tender-hearted. The trouble, really, might be Peter himself as much as anyone. His tearful remorse before the king suggested that he would take a long time to get the better of his own guilt. Until he did, he would be unfit for any duty that put him too close to the king or Princess Signy or Prince Kai.

He might just be perfect, on the other hand, for sitting in a cramped office, looking at pictures of a human woman who didn't even bear much resemblance to her royal sister.

If Tristan felt a moment's uneasiness at that thought— if his tiger, deep within, stirred and growled, tail-tip flicking—he pushed it aside. He had a mission; he had to have help to find Poppy Zlotsky as quickly as possible. The pictures of her were not his to guard jealously from anyone else, even if, for some strange reason, he wanted to.

~~*

11

Tristan had no trouble signing Peter out of the cells to keep under his own supervision—in fact, since he was technically taking over guarding Peter, he freed up a guardsman from monitoring him.

"Thanks," Fionn said, grinning widely as he gave an absent scratch to the back of his neck. "I'm gonna get a swim in before shift change, then. This schedule's been hell."

Tristan nodded to the young selkie, his own expression as flat as ever. Fionn's grin shrank to an awkward smile before he departed, and it occurred to Tristan that after all these years, he was unlikely to make another friend like Kai in the remaining ranks of the guardsmen.

But that was neither here nor there. Tristan had a mission to complete.

It was easy enough to explain to Peter what assistance he needed, and his hunch about Peter's familiarity with the human internet was confirmed immediately. "Did you check out the accounts of people who she's tagged, or people whose comments she replies to? If anybody's seen her recently, they might have put up a picture with her in it, even in the background or something. And even if she's only active on Insta, they might be on Twitter or Facebook, or..."

"Ah," Tristan said. "Yes, well, I thought that would get rather labor-intensive, with so many accounts to check."

Peter nodded quickly, darting a glance at his cheek and then meeting Tristan's eyes again. "Of course. I'll get right on it, sir."

Tristan nodded firmly and turned back to his computer. He pretended not to notice the way Peter kept looking at his new scars and then quickly away from them. He'd forgotten that the king and Princess Signy weren't the only ones Peter might feel guilty toward, but Tristan wasn't about to give up his assistant now that he had him.

It still took days of searching. No obvious friends— or... other attachments—stood out among Poppy's photographs and online interactions, but they developed a vast pool of acquaintances to check.

Early one evening, clicking through accounts while Peter frowned at a map, Tristan found himself suddenly face to face with Poppy again. She was wearing a brilliantly blue dress and a brilliant smile, standing with an arm around a woman in green. The photo was captioned, *Heading out for a night on the town! See you soon, guys!*

It had been posted only minutes earlier. His heart was suddenly beating fast, his fingers rising toward the screen before he jerked them back.

He'd found her. Now all he had to do was get to—his eyes scanned down the page, searching for more information—to London, and hope she stayed put for at least a few hours.

2

POPPY

Poppy Zlotsky had come to London to spend a little time on her own, to clear her head and consider what she really wanted to do next. For all that she still hadn't found the ineffable *something* she had been looking for this year— for her whole life—she was getting tired of chasing it. She just wanted to sit still and watch people go by and think about what it was she was looking for, and why she thought she was so different from all the people just going about their normal lives in one place day after day, like she had never managed to do for long.

So of course, she walked into a Pret a Manger to get a sandwich—in the City of London, the business district where she'd never spent any time and didn't know anyone—and immediately spotted Sasha Baird in line at the counter. Worse, Sasha spotted her at the same time, breaking into a huge grin and waving at Poppy.

Poppy couldn't help waving back, forcing a wide, bright smile.

Of course it would be Sasha, of all the people she could have run into. Poppy adored Sasha—you couldn't help loving Sasha, she was so sweet and kind-hearted. She was just also constantly in the process of stumbling from one disaster to another, and Poppy couldn't see a disaster unfolding without jumping in to help.

So much for a quiet week or two in a hostel, unplugging from everything and thinking things over.

Poppy felt like a jerk for thinking it in the next second, as Sasha hurried over, swinging her tray out of the way to enfold Poppy in a hug. Poppy hugged her back fiercely. One of the things she had been getting tired of lately was being alone all the time—even in a group, she was always separate somehow, the girl who was just passing through, the girl who was too smart and careful to mess around with strangers or let any guy tie her down. Sasha was a good friend, and Poppy was lucky to have friends to find in unexpected places.

Poppy drew back from the hug and noticed Sasha's neatly tailored work clothes as she excused herself to go buy lunch while Sasha found a table. She scolded herself more as she picked out a sandwich. Sasha was obviously here on her lunch break; she had a nice job in the city now. She was probably worrying about that poor Poppy Zlotsky who was basically homeless and wondering if Poppy was going to make her late getting back to work.

Not even minutes later, Sasha blew *that* idea out of the water.

"No," Poppy said. "No, Sasha, you *cannot* be thinking of getting back together with Daniel. When I met you you had broken up with him for the *third time* and you were hiding from him in *Nepal.*"

Sasha gave her that helpless pleading look Poppy knew all too well. "I know, I know, but he—"

"*No,*" Poppy repeated. "Sasha, unless he's joined a cult and been brainwashed into being a *decent human being* who won't try to make you *steal money from your parents when he's short on cash*—"

"And I wasn't *hiding* from him," Sasha added, but she

wouldn't meet Poppy's eyes now. "It's not like he was *abusive*, and that whole money thing was a misunderstanding—"

"Why," Poppy demanded, not bothering to argue the fine points. "Sasha, why on earth would you get back together with him?"

"He's really sorry this time, Poppy. He's changed, he's got a good job. He sent me the most gorgeous flowers, and..." Sasha mumbled the end of it into her straw.

Poppy narrowed her eyes. "What was that?"

"He wants to take me to Paris," Sasha repeated, slightly louder. "Tomorrow."

Poppy actually checked her phone to be sure. "Tomorrow is *Wednesday*, Sasha."

Sasha sat back with a sigh, her shoulders slumping. "I know, but I *hate* this job, and it's not going anywhere, so why—"

"Because it's *not going anywhere*," Poppy pointed out. "Unlike Daniel, who's going to whisk you off to Paris and then disappear for a month without calling, *like he's done before*. You'll be lucky if he brings you back to England first!"

Sasha sighed, finally meeting Poppy's eyes with an apologetic look. "I know! I know it's not a good idea, but he really wants to try again, and, I mean, what if this is it? What if he's the guy?"

"You would know by now if he was the guy," Poppy said firmly. Her romantic track record might be almost nonexistent—she never really stuck around long enough to be serious about anyone—but she was rock solid at knowing when a guy *wasn't* a good idea. It was obvious that, after three tries with this one, Sasha knew it too.

"You're just bored, and running off to Paris sounds exciting, but you know it would go the same way this time that it did the last three times."

"Four," Sasha muttered. "We hooked up last month, too."

17

Poppy shook her head. "Don't even drag this out, Sasha, just tell him no. Here, give me your phone, *I'll* tell him no."

Sasha handed over her phone and didn't bother telling Poppy what she would see: it was right there at the bottom of the message chain. *See you tonight!*

Poppy opened her mouth to scold Sasha again and winced, sitting back in her seat. "Sasha, really, are you in love with him? Do you actually want to get back together with him and run off to Paris together?"

Poppy thought for a guilty second of her sister, Signy, who had sent her a text out of the blue a couple of weeks earlier, saying that she had met a guy and was going off to Europe with him. The handful of texts that followed seemed to indicate Signy was happy with her choice—but then of course Signy had done the right thing. Signy *always* did the right thing. Poppy was the wild, careless one, always running off.

Sasha covered her face with her hands and shook her head. "I thought I was done with him, I was totally through, especially after last month. But I'm not seeing anyone else, and he promised to take me shopping, so I figured even if he's as much of an asshole as ever, at least I get a shopping trip in Paris out of it? But you're right, he would probably turn around and ask me to pay or just vanish and leave me there or something."

Poppy scrolled up through Sasha's texts, looking for how Daniel had gotten her so turned around this time. She frowned as she read.

"He's really not taking no for an answer, is he?"

Sasha groaned. "I know, I know, red flag."

"True, but..." Poppy kept scrolling. "I mean, he's really specifically determined to take you to Paris *tomorrow*. Like. I think this is something *shady*, Sasha, like he has to be in Paris tomorrow for something, and—"

Sasha got a weird look on her face and took a hasty bite of her sandwich.

Poppy took a bite of her own lunch and stared Sasha down.

"He didn't just send me flowers," Sasha admitted. "He sent me a new bag, too. And he told me that with traveling last minute, we might not have seats together. And he always gets hassled, so I should probably go through security separately."

Poppy put a hand over her mouth to keep from yelling out loud in the middle of the café. When she could control her voice she whispered, "Sasha! That is *so many red flags*. There are no red flags left for anything else! He used all of them!"

"I know," Sasha repeated, in the same tone as she'd used before, and then she stopped, her eyes going wide. Poppy could see the second when she flipped from feeling dumb about this to feeling *scared*, and she almost wanted to take it back, except that she had a feeling Sasha was right.

Sasha leaned toward her, her gaze darting around like Daniel might have suddenly materialized in the café. "Oh my God, Pops, do you think he could be *dangerous*? If—like if I said no now, would he…"

Poppy set Sasha's phone down and closed her hand over Sasha's. "Hey. Probably not, okay? He would probably just be a jerk about it."

Sasha didn't quit looking scared, though.

"Okay, look, you should go tonight, so he doesn't think anything's wrong," Poppy said, the plan coming to her as she spoke. "But I'll come with. And I'll see if I can't get him interested in me, right? See if he'll invite me to Paris instead, get his attention off you. Then you can dump him for being a complete hound, go straight from the club to a train somewhere else—your aunt lives up north, right?"

Sasha nodded, the fear in her eyes fading as she got drawn into Poppy's plan. Poppy felt a little bad about that—what if she was just like Daniel, convincing Sasha to do what *she* wanted? Except that all Poppy wanted out of this was to help Sasha, unlike Daniel, who apparently wanted to do something illegal and maybe dangerous.

"Whatever's happening is happening tomorrow, so after that he probably won't care anymore," Poppy went on. "You can come back tomorrow night, block his number, move on."

Sasha nodded, then frowned. "But—wait, Poppy, *you're* not going to go to Paris with him, right?"

"Of course not," Poppy assured her. "I'll handle that part, don't you worry."

Sasha grinned. "Of course you will. You always do, don't you? You never need anyone to bail you out of anything."

Poppy smiled back. It wouldn't do any good to let Sasha see that she had no idea how she was going to handle a guy like Daniel, or that she was getting tired of handling everything on her own. She couldn't let Sasha down, so Poppy would just have to think of something.

~~*

Getting Daniel's attention turned out to be no problem at all. As soon as he spotted Sasha and Poppy together, he zeroed in on Poppy and all but ignored Sasha. Poppy saw the amusement in his eyes every time Sasha tried to get his attention and knew that it wasn't *just* that he was a dog, blatantly flirting with someone new while Sasha watched. Daniel was doing it on purpose to punish Sasha for bringing along a friend on what was supposed to be a date.

Even knowing that cutting Sasha out was the whole point, Poppy couldn't help feeling rude ignoring her. She angled herself partially away from Daniel on the little couch he'd maneuvered them to in a dark corner of the club. "So, Paris tomorrow, huh? Are you all packed? Leaving bright and early?"

Daniel gave a nasty little laugh. "Sasha's not the bright-and-early type, poppet."

Poppy gritted her teeth to keep from reacting to the

nickname she hated most.

"In fact, I expect an early bird could cut her out entirely," Daniel added, sliding an arm around Poppy's waist and tugging her close. "You're a lively one, now. How'd you like to take a little jaunt with me tomorrow?"

Poppy did a pretty good wide-eyed *who me?* look, and she turned it on full force. "What, you mean... but Sasha—"

"No, you know what, I've had enough of this," Sasha stood up. She sounded more hurt than angry, her bravado obvious, but that was all right, Poppy thought. No more than Daniel would expect, and once Sasha was out of this the first half of the plan would have worked. "Go to Paris with him, Poppy, just don't ever tell me how it went. I'm through with both of you, you're welcome to each other."

"Sasha," Poppy tugged against Daniel's grip, making to rise as Sasha stalked away, but Daniel held her in place with an iron grip. Poppy fought down a nasty squirm of fear.

"Oh, no, poppet, you're not going anywhere," Daniel murmured. "Except to Paris, with me, like I said. You poach your friend's man, you'd better stick with him for at least a day. Well, or a night."

Poppy made herself be still, made herself smile. She had to give Sasha time to get away from here—an hour or two, at least, before she could try to extricate herself.

"All right," Poppy said, turning a smile on Daniel. "But you'd better be able to keep up with me on the dance floor, then."

"Oh, I think you'll find I can keep up with you anywhere," Daniel growled, no hint of humor in his voice. But he let her stand, even if he didn't let her out of arm's reach.

Poppy knew it was an illusion, but she felt safer with other people crowding around them. She let herself slide into the rhythm of music that was more a physical force than a sound, almost too loud to hear anything but the

21

beat. As long as she could stay out here, as long as the music was playing, all Poppy had to do was dance.

She just had to give Sasha enough time to get away, and then figure out how to get away herself. A chance would turn up. Something always turned up. She'd just have to keep her eyes open.

But that would be later. For now, all she needed was the music and the crowd.

3

TRISTAN

Tristan watched Peter stare into a laptop for the entire flight to London. He was convinced that he could determine what actual establishment Miss Zlotsky and her friend, Miss *sallybird1995*, were visiting tonight.

Tristan had only touched down briefly in London a few times before, but he knew that the city held more people than all of Valtyra. They'd likely have to call on diplomatic assistance to connect with the local police, monitor information on airline passengers, circulate photographs, wade through hours of CCTV footage.

But as they were descending toward Heathrow, Peter said, "I found them! I know what club they're at."

He gave Tristan a look of hopeful almost-pride; if Tristan were the sort of person who could, this would be the time for a smile, or perhaps to squeeze his shoulder, to encourage him.

Tristan couldn't do anything but say, "Good. Figure out our fastest route there once we're on the ground."

Peter's smile faltered, and he cast a long, guilty look at Tristan's scarred cheek before he bent his head over the computer again.

Tristan looked away, though he was quite sure his own face would betray nothing of his awareness of having made a bad mistake. He had brought Peter on this trip in hopes of boosting his confidence, giving him a chance to feel that he had redeemed himself from his earlier terrible mistake. He would only make it worse, though, if he could do nothing but convince Peter that he still held a grudge.

Well, at least Peter might be useful in persuading Poppy to accompany them, since there could be no doubt that she would dismiss Tristan from her bright and shining attention at once.

The last miles of the trip stretched an agonizingly long time; even with their diplomatic credentials speeding them through the customs formalities, it took the better part of an hour to escape the airport and board the train Peter insisted was their quickest option.

"Oh, no, they've split up," Peter said, frowning into his phone. "Sasha's..."

Tristan raised his eyebrows slightly. It took a moment for Peter to notice his scrutiny and look up; he winced when he did.

"I was tracking Miss Zlotsky's friend," he explained, a nervous flush rising on his cheeks, his hands shaking slightly as he tapped at the screen. "But they've... had some kind of falling-out, I think. From what I can tell, Miss Zlotsky remained at the club."

Tristan nodded briskly.

Peter went back to staring into his phone, chewing his lower lip and making quick taps and swipes, becoming calmer the longer he went without having to look at Tristan.

Tristan guided him by the shoulder when it came time to change trains and again when they emerged onto the street. People were everywhere, despite the late hour, and music poured out of a dozen different clubs along this stretch. Tristan struggled to filter out the noise, to focus his preternatural shifter's senses on scanning for a slim redheaded woman amid the throng, a voice that sounded like the recordings he had heard of Poppy Zlotsky.

"It's this way," Peter said, finally looking up from the phone in his hand. Tristan released his grip on Peter's shoulder and stayed close at his side as he led the way; he did seem confident enough when he had a task, at least.

Suddenly a single voice seemed to ring out over all the noise.

"Okay, okay! I just thought we were having a good time dancing."

Poppy Zlotsky. Tristan turned his head, wishing he had his tiger's mobile ears to better focus on the sound. He was barely aware of Peter beside him, utterly attuned to that voice.

Tristan turned and jogged across the street, listening for that voice as he dodged through traffic, barely hearing the blares of car horns and shouts of drivers. Peter was only a step behind him as he reached the opposite side of the street, and he caught Tristan's arm as they stepped onto the pavement.

"Stay here," Tristan said, shaking off Peter's grip and keeping his eyes on the door of the club Poppy's voice had emanated from. "If she gets past me, trail her."

Peter nodded hastily, shoving his phone into his pocket, and Tristan started up a half-flight of stairs toward the doors. The place was busy; there were a handful of other people heading toward the doors, and a double handful coming out, but they all made way for him.

He stopped at the top of the stairs when he caught sight of a tumble of brilliant copper hair; Poppy was being towed along by a tall man in dark clothes. His build was big and broad, and Tristan tallied the few scars he could see, half-glimpsed tattoos, and combined them with the way he moved and the cold look in his eyes and knew that this man was dangerous.

For a human, anyway. Tristan didn't think he would

have any trouble with him.

He returned his gaze to Miss Zlotsky, intending to double-check his first assessment that she was not altogether pleased to be in the man's company, but this time they were close enough that she could see Tristan. Their eyes met.

It struck him like a storm wave out of nowhere, like a sudden impact from something as unyielding as a mountainside. He had found Poppy Zlotsky.

And she was his mate.

Tristan knew that his expression would reveal nothing, though his tiger roared within him, calling out for his mate. Tristan tore his gaze from her eyes to spot the grip her unwelcome companion had on her arm. When he glanced up to Poppy's face again, she was still looking at him; as she reached the threshold she set her feet against the man's pull and turned a dramatic frown on Tristan.

"Did my sister send you?"

Tristan was taken aback, but betrayed nothing. "Yes, Miss, so if you would come with me..."

"What the hell is this?" The man with her jerked at her arm.

"Sorry, Daniel, my sister must have hired him, she—it's a long story, but she's crazy overprotective sometimes," Poppy said. "It's easier if I just let this guy take me to see her so she doesn't freak out."

Poppy, Tristan realized after a fraction of a second, was *improvising.* Of course she had no idea who he was. Signy hadn't hired him, and certainly had never been in any position to send anyone after her before. But Tristan's formal attire and professional bearing made the story plausible.

He gave a faint bow, making his face even more inscrutable, and repeated, "Miss."

"Who the fuck are you, cuttin' in on my patch?" Daniel demanded, stepping up to Tristan, which only made it obvious that some of the miasma of alcohol on the air was definitely coming from him. It also made it clear that Tristan was a few inches taller and had no intention of stepping back to give the man room.

Tristan raised his eyebrows very slightly, letting his tiger's utter unconcern with any human's posturing show through. Daniel's eyes darted down to the scars on his cheek and throat, and he let go of Poppy's arm with an abrupt motion, nearly shoving her away. Tristan offered one hand, but she steadied herself without it.

"Do what you like, poppet," Daniel snapped. "But if you want in on that trip, give me your number—or is your *sister* going to forbid you to travel, too?"

"No, no, of course not, I'd never let her!" Poppy made a show of enthusiasm that might have persuaded a human's drink-dulled senses, but was obvious to Tristan as a lie. His tiger growled in satisfaction while Poppy turned on her phone and allowed Daniel to send himself a text from it. "See you in the morning—bright and early! I've got to pack, anyway."

That sounded slightly less like a lie, but Poppy reclaimed her phone and stepped closer to Tristan.

Daniel sneered, "No point leaving just yet, then," and turned away, staggering back into the club.

Tristan turned toward Poppy—*his mate, his to protect, his, human and American and perfect*—and offered her his arm. "Miss?"

Poppy giggled a little, sounding suddenly drunk though he couldn't smell anything on her. She put one hand to her forehead and took his arm with the other, allowing him to guide her down the stairs. "Thanks. Sir."

Her closeness, her touch, was intoxicating, and he should have pulled her to him, should have spoken odes to her beauty. Instead, he said expressionlessly, "Tristan."

They were back down to the pavement then; he looked around and glimpsed Peter watching them from several meters away.

"Hi, Tristan, I'm Poppy," she said, looking around

distractedly, everywhere but at him. "Could you possibly just walk me a little further away?"

Anywhere, on my knees, if you ask it of me.

But of course he couldn't say that. Tristan merely nodded and drew her slightly closer, guiding her along with the flow of pedestrians. They passed Peter, and Tristan was distantly aware of the young guardsman falling in behind them, but it was hard to care about anything but Poppy's presence at his side, the touch of her hand on his arm through the layers of his clothes.

Poppy, however, was tense and watchful at his side. It was obvious that she was not at all sure that she had entirely escaped Daniel, and that she had no glimmer of awareness of what Tristan was to her.

Humans often didn't. That was supposed to be one of the many ways in which humans were inferior. They could be deceived; they could be utterly unaware of the perfect mate who stood before them.

Tristan's tiger longed to make her aware, to leave her in no doubt that they could and would protect her, keep her, make a home for her... But Tristan had learned control long ago, and even now, in the presence of his mate, he had no idea how to loosen it.

If it was true that a human mate could not recognize the shifter she was destined for, it was equally true that the shifter in question had a responsibility to tell her the truth and let her make up her own mind. More, he had an opportunity to make that truth something she might be pleased by, rather than an ultimatum at first sight. Poppy could *choose* him, if she wished to; he would not simply stand before her like so many shifters he'd seen, finding their mates at arranged mixers, and be accepted because neither of them had any choice in the matter.

But that meant he must, somehow, find the way to woo Poppy—while protecting her, and without forcing her to do anything or go anywhere, and without telling her too much truth, yet without lying to her. And he had two weeks before the royal wedding.

But he had found her. He had found his *mate*. He had given up on any thought of ever finding his mate after he abandoned his family, rejecting all their best efforts to find him a shifter bride. He had taught himself not to think of it, not to imagine a future beyond the Royal Guard, but now...

Now he was on a crowded street with Poppy and she still didn't know who he was—didn't know any of the many things she would have to know about him. And he had no idea how he would ever persuade her to listen to even the least part of that. He couldn't run ahead of himself.

Poppy had stopped looking around and was looking down at her feet instead, leaning minutely against Tristan. Her grip on his arm tightened, then loosened, and he realized she was shivering.

"Poppy? Are you—"

Poppy wobbled, swaying into him.

Tristan took the liberty of curling his arm around her, almost carrying her as he guided her out of the flow of pedestrian traffic to a little stretch of open curb. She was almost boneless by the time he got her to a sitting position, and he knelt beside her, guiding her head down to her knees.

He looked around hastily for Peter, who was holding his phone and looking nearly as pale as Poppy likely was, his expression a portrait of worry for her. Tristan knew his own expression must look as if he didn't care at all.

Tristan shook his head slightly, to tell Peter there was no need. Poppy was breathing steadily, and he had a feeling he knew what this was.

"It's all right," he said, resting his hand carefully on the middle of her back, trying to make his level voice low and reassuring. "Just keep breathing. You're safe now."

"I didn't," Poppy said, a little muffled as she still had her head down. "He didn't do anything to me."

Tristan glanced at the reddened mark where the man had been gripping her arm; she was fair, and likely bruised easily. But the physical was the least of it sometimes. Tristan's father had never struck him, and still Tristan had turned himself to stone to keep himself safe.

"He didn't have to hurt you for you to know he was dangerous," Tristan said plainly. If a tactical assessment was all he could give her, at least he could say that. "You held it together very well until you were safely away from him. You can take a moment to react now."

"Thanks," Poppy said, a little edge in her voice that Tristan couldn't quite read. She was shivering harder now, her arms tight around her own waist. He could see goosebumps down her bare arms despite the mildness of the night.

He took his hand from her back and shrugged quickly out of his coat. "Here. You're cold, take my coat for a moment."

He laid it over her when she didn't object; she huddled down a little more, but didn't push it away, so he let himself believe it was some comfort to her. If it was terribly satisfying to his tiger to know that she was sheltered under his clothing, breathing in his scent... well, even a flood watered someone's fields.

"Thanks," Poppy repeated after a few minutes, turning her head to peer out at Tristan over the collar of his jacket. "You—were you meeting people? You don't have to sit here with me all night."

"My plans are flexible," Tristan said calmly, fighting the rush of desire that came with meeting his mate's eyes again and knowing that she really saw *him* this time, not just a means of escape. *Yes, yes, look at me, see me.* "I don't mind sitting here with you, at least until you're able to stand."

Poppy moved her feet as though she were going to try it, and Tristan put his hand on her shoulder through the muffling layer of his coat. "I don't want to have to catch you again. Wait a little longer."

He saw the impulse to do it precisely because he had told her not to flash across Poppy's face and braced himself to find some way of persuading her without frightening her.

But then Poppy nodded and closed her eyes, putting her head down again. Tristan felt a warm flash of pride all out of proportion. She'd listened to him, she'd heard him. *His mate.*

"The last time this happened to me I almost drowned," Poppy said.

Tristan's grip tightened a little. He had a sudden, new horror of everything that could have happened before he found her, anytime in the last year.

"Beforehand, I mean," Poppy went on. "I managed to get out of the water and I walked up to the top of the beach and then I was just sitting in the sand shaking. I don't know how long it lasted. I wasn't really.... I was by myself. So I don't know."

His tiger lashed its tail, growling miserably at the thought of Poppy going through anything like that alone, with no one to watch over her, no one to hold her and tell her how glad they were that she had survived. Even if Tristan couldn't say it properly, or make his face show it, at least he was here with her.

"You're not alone now," Tristan promised her quietly. "We can stay here as long as you need."

Poppy nodded, and instead of thanking him again, she leaned toward him. Tristan closed his eyes and held still. If all she saw, or needed, was a rock to lean on—at least he was good at that.

She could lean on him as long as she needed to. Nothing mattered more than letting her do this in her own time.

4

POPPY

Poppy wondered if she could just live the rest of her life right here, sitting on a curb in London with a gorgeous stranger's suit coat draped over her shoulders. The delayed adrenaline reaction was wearing off, leaving her feeling tired and silly.

Except the guy—Tristan? She hoped she had heard that right, because she already liked the feel of it in her mouth—was still sitting quietly beside her. Letting her lean on him, letting her wear his coat, his hand resting lightly on her back. He didn't fidget, didn't show the least sign of being uncomfortable or wanting to get on with his night. Somehow she thought that he genuinely would just stay there, sitting beside her, all night if she didn't move.

So then she would never have to look him in the eye, or explain anything. She wouldn't have to strike up some kind of sane conversation, or beg a cool, collected stranger to meet her for coffee sometime when she wasn't in the middle of such a mess.

Her phone vibrated, and Poppy opened one eye to confirm that she had managed to hang on to her purse

33

through all of that. It was between her feet now. She could feel the muffled buzz when it repeated.

It had to be Daniel. The phone was an old one of Sasha's, and Poppy had bought a new SIM card for it today, putting it on a prepaid plan. She had given Sasha the number, just in case, but Sasha had already texted her to say she was safely on the train out of town.

Daniel, on the other hand, would probably text her all night.

Poppy gave in to the temptation to nestle a little closer to Tristan.

"Do you want me to turn your phone off?" Tristan murmured.

She glanced up at him without thinking, startled that he could hear the vibration from where he sat.

As soon as she met his eyes she forgot all about her phone. Tristan's eyes were a clear, pale amber, fringed in long black lashes. His hair was black too, a tousle of loose curls that she wanted to run her fingers through. He had the clear brown skin and fine features of a Bollywood star, except that his left cheek was marred with two parallel red scars.

He knew what danger was. He had survived something. And when Poppy had needed a way out, he was right there, following her lead without hesitation and somehow making Daniel back down without saying a word or raising a hand. Through all of it he had been calm and steady, letting her hang off of him, lean on him.

And maybe she should back off a little, but she didn't want to at all. Poppy didn't think she'd ever been this close to someone this hot.

"Poppy?" Tristan prompted, still looking serious and calm, not impatient or amused at her mind wandering. She remembered that he had asked her about her phone.

She shook her head, shifting her feet away from it as she looked down. "No. It's fine, I... have to do something about him, sooner or later."

"But not right now," Tristan assured her. "Right now we can just sit."

Poppy nodded. It finally occurred to her that he had an accent that wasn't quite like the others she was accustomed to hearing. His English was perfect, but his faint accent wasn't any kind of British she'd heard before, wasn't one of the accents she'd heard before from south Asia or Africa, which she might have expected from his looks. It was... Scandinavian?

She liked it, whatever it was. She wanted him to keep talking to her all night.

She carefully didn't think about what she'd like to hear him saying.

Sitting on the ground was starting to get old, though. And they weren't that far from the club where she'd left Daniel. She didn't doubt Tristan could get him to back off again—but what if Daniel showed up with a bunch of equally shady friends? Even if no one got hurt, Poppy didn't want to see him again tonight, or ever.

But if she didn't show up tomorrow...

She pushed the thought away. *Not right now*, like Tristan had said.

"I think..." Poppy sat up a little straighter, shrugging her shoulders to resettle the weight of his coat. It sent up a little waft of warmth and she realized she could smell him on it; the faint, spicy scent shot heat through her whole body.

Tristan studied her face, then nodded. "You've got some color, at least."

"Well, by my standards," Poppy said, touching the back of one hand to her cheek to be sure she wasn't beet red.

"Naturally," Tristan agreed, and the corner of his mouth turned up, a tiny fraction of a style that was still somehow breathtaking. "I'm used to making allowances for you pale types."

He stood up then, stepping into the street so that he could stand facing her as he offered both his hands. Poppy laid both of hers in them, noticing how much smaller they were, as well as paler. He left his hands open, so it was up to her to hold on, and he let her pull against him, levering herself up to her feet.

"Oh," Poppy said when she was standing, feeling a little rush of dizziness. "Oh, you're really *tall*."

Tristan blinked at her, and after a few seconds, *both* sides of his mouth turned up in a tiny, tiny smile; she thought it must be like getting a belly laugh out of anyone else, and it made her feel warm all the way through. Poppy clung to his hands, thrown by how much she wanted to make him smile, how much she wanted to know what was behind that cool, quiet exterior.

She giggled a little at her own inanity. She had to be making an *amazing* first impression right now; a serious guy like Tristan probably *loved* party girls who couldn't even walk half a block in a straight line. "Sorry, that's—I just—"

"Quite all right," Tristan assured her. He tugged one hand free of hers and adjusted the hang of his coat on her shoulders, making no move to take it back. "I could say that your hair is really very red, if you like."

"Yeah, I'm red all over," Poppy replied, and then flushed. Now he really would think she was a party girl, or maybe just drunk. The flirtatious answer had been automatic, but she had never said it to anyone as gorgeous and kind and—and *tall*—as Tristan. It suddenly mattered very much what he said back.

Tristan didn't laugh. He took one hand from around hers to tuck a lock of hair behind her ear. "Would you care to walk a little farther, Miss? Or... catch a cab, perhaps?"

"It's Poppy," Poppy corrected firmly, then smiled as she added, "unless you want me to call you Mister."

Tristan shook his head. "Tristan is... quite enough. Poppy."

Poppy nodded and looked around. If Tristan hadn't helped her get free of Daniel, she'd entertained visions of just running from him. It would still be best to get farther away.

"It would be my honor to see you home safely," Tristan said, like that was... just a thing people said. But it didn't sound artificial, from him; Tristan seemed like someone who knew something about honor. "We should be able to get a cab on the corner."

"I..." Poppy squeezed his hand tight. "I don't want to be alone."

Tristan nodded, as though she hadn't said anything strange, or anything he was going to dismiss as a drunk girl freaking out. "Then you won't be. Come, this way."

He guided Poppy back up onto the pavement, and they walked hand in hand toward a larger street. Tristan seemed to make a black cab appear just by raising his hand for it, and he handed her into the back seat like she was wearing a ball gown instead of the one cute dress that never wrinkled in her pack. Plus his suit coat.

She took a moment to slip her arms into the sleeves as she scooted across the back seat, making room for him, only to realize that the sleeves covered her hands completely. The heavy wool of the coat didn't scrunch up easily.

Tristan settled beside her, pulling the door shut and making the whole world seem to disappear—except for the cabbie, on the other side of the partition. When he asked where they were going, Tristan looked at her.

Poppy's hands curled into fists in the sleeves of Tristan's coat. Tristan had offered to see her home, which... was nowhere, really, in the long run. But for tonight it was her hostel in the City of London, which would be a ghost town right now. She'd have to slip into the crowded dormitory in the dark to find her things, to shower the smell of the club and the memory of Daniel's touch off her skin.

But she needed her things, so that was where she had to go next, even if she didn't want to stay there tonight. She rattled off the address of the hostel, and the cabbie nodded and pulled out into traffic.

Tristan reached out, his hands hovering above hers where they were lost in the sleeves of his coat. "May I?"

Poppy nodded, watching as Tristan carefully turned the stiff fabric back on itself, revealing the satiny lining underneath and, eventually, her hands.

"Thank you," she said. "Did I say that, before? Thank you for playing along. I don't know what I would have done if I hadn't spotted someone I could..."

Poppy trailed off, leaving the last word unspoken. *Someone I could trust.*

It was true. She didn't know *why*, exactly, but she had known as soon as she saw Tristan looking at her, standing so still on the threshold of the club in his crisp black suit, that she could trust him. She rarely had *that* kind of intuition about anyone—her assessments of strange men usually ranged from "not immediately dangerous, wait and see" to "*RUN*"—but Tristan was different somehow, quite aside from his looks.

"You did," Tristan said. "You thanked me repeatedly. But think nothing of it. I'm sure you would do the same for someone in a tight spot, wouldn't you?"

Poppy shrugged, looking away. That was exactly why *she* had been in the tight spot, of course. But she wasn't used to anyone else being around to help her, or looking at her like they saw more in her than an aimless American girl.

"May I ask," Tristan said slowly. "Why did you say what you said, when you saw me? You asked if your sister had sent me."

"Oh," Poppy tilted her head back, leaning against the seat and wrapping Tristan's coat around her like armor. "It was... the word *sister* disarms a lot of guys. It's the least likely connection to make a guy like Daniel flip out, but it also doesn't suggest too much to—"

"To me," Tristan said, his face turning really expressionless as he looked away. "I see."

38

"No, I," Poppy twisted toward him, reaching out to grab one of his hands with hers. Her bare knee rested on top of his, and she felt Tristan go very still beside her. His hand was warm under hers, and as soon as she touched him she didn't want to ever stop. "I just, I mean, in the first second—"

Tristan gave her another tiny fraction of a smile, raising the hand she hadn't grabbed to tuck back her hair, though it hadn't fallen down. His fingers grazed the rim of her ear, brushed against the corner of her jaw. "I understand, Poppy. It was clever. And I suppose I couldn't have passed as your brother without a great many explanations."

Poppy nodded, letting herself grin now that he had smiled. "If you'd been a redhead, I might have tried that. But brothers fight over their sisters sometimes, and I didn't want a fight. I just wanted to get out of there."

Tristan nodded. "Very clever. You're a strategic thinker."

Poppy tilted her head, wanting to deflect his quiet, factual praise even though it warmed her inside that he saw something like that in her, something real. "I have to be. You'd be surprised how many tricks women have, especially the ones who run around alone with no brothers to fight our battles for us."

"Less surprised now that I've met you." Tristan's eyes stayed steady on her, and she wouldn't have been at all surprised if he'd pulled a Sherlock Holmes right then and told her her whole life story right then. She felt as if she were under a microscope.

Poppy ducked her head, trying to hide her smile. Tristan's hand turned under hers, holding on, and Poppy curled closer to him, resting her forehead against his shoulder. She could feel the heat of his body through the thin dress shirt, and she breathed in the starchy clean smell of his clothes. She wanted so much more than this, but she was also tired, and still coming down from her narrow escape. This was good, too.

"Do you really have a sister, then?" He asked. "Or does she only exist for strategic purposes?"

Poppy winced, unseen. "No, she's real. I mean, she doesn't send people to check up on me, but I have an older sister. Siggy. She's the responsible one. Usually, anyway. She met some guy a few weeks ago and ran off to Europe with him."

"Ah," Tristan said. "That does sound rather... reckless."

Poppy shook her head, feeling a guilty twinge; she didn't want to make Signy sound bad, and she had a feeling *reckless* was about the worst thing Tristan could think of anyone. "She sounded happy, the texts she sent me about it. They were staying someplace with this great ocean view, and..."

Poppy swallowed hard. She felt stupidly close to crying, in the back of a cab with some guy she hadn't known for an hour. At least she could blame the adrenaline if Tristan saw, but it was still not the first impression she wanted to make on this dashing stranger.

Was that what this was? Did she just want what her sister had? But no—just wanting a great guy couldn't have magically summoned Tristan into existence. Maybe she wouldn't have been so eager to stay near him, wouldn't have found herself imagining a real relationship with him, without Signy's example, but Tristan himself was entirely real.

"Did she stop texting you?" Tristan asked softly. He was running his fingers over her hair again, and she closed her eyes and let him, nestling closer like a cat asking to be petted.

"No, I turned my phone off," Poppy admitted. "I just knew if I left it on the next thing I'd get from her would be a wedding invitation or something. That's the thing about Signy, she *always* does the right thing. Mom and Dad moved us all over the country, but Signy was the one who kept track of all our school records. Signy stayed by herself for two months after the rest of us left, so she could finish high school on time. If Signy ran off with this guy, I don't doubt she's gonna live happily ever after with him in some little stone house by the sea, having a dozen perfect little babies."

Poppy blinked rapidly to hold back the tears that threatened.

"I just," Poppy said. "I know she... she would tell me to visit or something. But it wouldn't be mine, you know? And she wouldn't say, see, Poppy, all you have to do is meet the most perfect guy in the world and then you could be happy too, but..."

Tristan kept petting her hair. He didn't ask anything else, but somehow Poppy thought he understood.

"I just wanted to figure it out for myself," Poppy whispered. "Maybe that's stupid, but I just—I just want to find something for myself. Something that's mine. Something I did first."

She forced a little laugh and shook her head. "Sorry. I sound like a bitch when I talk about her. She's great, I just—"

"You don't," Tristan said softly. He turned a little, tapping his fingers under Poppy's chin. She looked up and met his eyes, feeling a little thrill at the way he looked back at her, unwavering even when she couldn't help getting emotional. "You sound like you're looking for something very important. You have a right to try to find it. I hope you do."

"I think I'm getting close," Poppy said softly, and then the cab came to a hard stop.

Poppy looked outside and realized they'd arrived at the hostel, in a narrow lane near St. Paul's Cathedral. "Oh, I—this is me, but—"

What could she do? Invite Tristan into a darkened dormitory or a shabby common room? She looked at him, and found him studying the hostel with a slight frown. It struck her, just then, that he was older than she was—not *old*, obviously, there were no real lines on his face and his

41

black hair didn't show a single thread of gray—but a proper, serious adult. He no doubt stayed in nice hotels when he traveled, not hostels or the couches of friends-of-friends.

She looked down at the turned-back sleeves of his suit coat and realized they were probably *really nice* hotels.

"Poppy," he said quietly. "Are you sure you'll be safe here?"

Poppy opened her mouth to say that of course she would—there were people around, and Daniel had no idea where she was staying. She knew how to take care of herself. She always did.

Before she could speak, Tristan added, just as seriously, as though it really mattered, "Will you *feel* safe here?"

She pictured lying awake among strangers, her phone buzzing and buzzing all night, and slowly shook her head. "But I—"

Tristan covered her hand with his. "If you wanted company, I swear I wouldn't expect anything. You could come to my hotel."

Poppy was nodding almost before Tristan finished speaking, her cheeks flushing hot as she realized that even if *Tristan* didn't expect anything to happen, she did. Or, well, she *wanted* something to happen; she didn't know quite how good her odds were yet. It was hard to know if Tristan just went around taking people seriously all the time, or if he was... actually serious about Poppy, especially.

"Will you wait?" She asked, glancing toward the cabbie, who was watching them with raised eyebrows.

"Of course," Tristan said firmly, and he opened the door and stepped out gracefully, keeping one hand on hers to assist her onto the ancient cobblestones.

"One minute," Poppy promised, and hurried over to the door to let herself in.

It took longer than a minute, of course. Fumbling in the dark to make sure she had all her things, she wound up pulling out the phone from her purse to use as a flashlight—which meant seeing the messages she'd gotten while she was with Tristan.

Only one of them was from Daniel: *Bright and early, poppet.*

There were three from Sasha, though. *Pops? Why is Daniel texting me??* and *Aren't you going? You said you would go?* and *He says you ditched him for a scarfaced guy in a suit? DEETS!*

Poppy closed all the messages and zipped up her pack, shoving the phone into her bag. Sasha was safe. Sasha was on a train, away from Daniel. There was no way Daniel would lure her back to the city, or find out where she was. There was no way Poppy was going to Paris, or anywhere, with Daniel. She had done her good deed and lived to tell the tale and she had met an *amazing* guy. She was done with this whole night.

She slung her pack on her shoulder, shoved the phone back into her purse, and hurried through checking out. The hostel clerk shot a curious look at the juxtaposition of her dress, her battered hiking pack, and Tristan's suit coat. Poppy pretended not to notice, though she felt her face heat a little anyway; she was never going to have a poker face like Tristan's.

Less than ten minutes later she was back out in the lane. Tristan was waiting for her, standing beside the open back door of the cab. He had rolled up the sleeves of his white shirt, and Poppy couldn't help staring at the muscles of his forearms as he handed her into the cab again and slid in to sit beside her.

She didn't let go after he settled in beside her, and Tristan gave her hand a squeeze. The cab got into motion as soon as he pulled the door shut; he must have already told the cabbie where they were going. Poppy glanced at the meter and saw that it had started over—clearly Tristan had already paid for their trip so far, which might explain why the cabbie was cooperating with all of this.

Poppy curled toward Tristan again, studying his profile as he watched the city go by. He was on his guard in a way Poppy tried to be in strange places; something about the quickness of his moving gaze told her that he knew what he was looking for. She thought of the scars on his face, his faint strange accent, his gorgeously tailored suit, his cool, calm self-control, and leaned close to his ear.

She felt him go a different kind of still just before she whispered, "Are you a spy, Tristan?"

Tristan turned his head, and they were kissing-close. She had the faintest impression of a smile from the corners of his eyes, but no more. "I believe there is a traditional answer to that question."

Poppy nodded, smiling a little herself, even though she didn't entirely think either of them was joking. "You could tell me, but then you'd have to kill me."

Tristan tilted his head slightly, not a nod but a gesture in that direction. "But we don't have to worry about that, because I am certainly not a spy."

"Of course not," Poppy agreed, trying to match his even tone. "That would be crazy."

"Well," Tristan said. "It would likely mean I wasn't very good at my job, if I could be identified so easily and meant not to be. But you are correct that I am an agent of my government, and that I am currently engaged in a highly sensitive and somewhat secret mission."

Poppy's mouth fell open. "That's... not the answer I was expecting."

Tristan did one of his tiny corner-of-the-mouth smiles. "Nothing you've said tonight has been what I was expecting, so that seems fair."

Poppy sat back, opening up a few inches between them. "You're serious?"

Tristan nodded and tapped one hand so lightly against the lapel of his coat that it couldn't possibly be mistaken for an attempt to touch her body beneath it. "Check for yourself. I travel on a diplomatic passport."

Poppy sat back all the way and reached into Tristan's suit jacket. Had he honestly let her out of his sight with his *passport* as well as his expensive suit coat? He didn't seem like the type to trust random girls that much.

Her fingers touched a familiar little booklet, and she pulled it out and stared at the seal on the cover. "Denmark?"

Tristan arched his eyebrows slightly. Poppy flipped the passport open on a picture of a somewhat younger Tristan, his black hair cut severely short so that no curls showed. His face was perfectly smooth, unmarked by the bright new scars across his cheek.

His full name was... *Tristan.*

"You only have one name? Like Cher?" She flipped through the pages of the passport, taking in the special stamps and notes that stated his diplomatic immunity.

"That's the only one I'm allowed to tell anyone, for as long as I stay in my current job," Tristan explained, and Poppy looked up sharply.

He was absolutely serious, his gaze intent on her. "Due to my particular duties, the oaths I've taken, and the nature of my present mission, I'm afraid there are many things—important things—that I can't tell you about myself and what I'm doing here."

Poppy frowned. "You said it was... somewhat secret. What does *that* mean? Is that like, two steps down from Top Secret?"

Tristan shook his head. "It's not an official classification. The mission isn't intrinsically secret—I'll be happy to explain it to you fully, once it's over—but for the time being, until I have a better idea of how things are going to play out, I have to keep the details close. Naturally, I'll understand if you're not comfortable being alone with me, knowing that there are things I have to keep from you."

Poppy looked down and flipped through the passport again. There were only a handful of stamps in it—entry and exit from England, entry and exit from Norway, and, just a couple of weeks ago, entry and exit from the United States. It was right around the time Signy had met her European dream guy and run off with him.

Poppy was tempted for a moment to ask if he knew a guy named Kai, if he really *did* know her sister.

But if she had a Euro for every person who'd demanded to know whether she knew some other random American, she'd never have to sleep in a hostel again. Coincidences happened, sure—look at how her day had started, stumbling over Sasha in the last place Poppy would have expected to find her—but Poppy's luck had never sent her anyone like Tristan before.

She turned back to the first page, the picture of Tristan taken more than ten years ago, according to the issue date of the passport. Nothing about it rang false to her. Nothing about *Tristan* seemed false. When he told her he was a secret agent, he made it sound like a mildly unusual civil service job, not some grandiose James Bond fantasy.

She looked him over again. "You don't carry a gun."

Tristan's micro-smile was more like the very tiniest smirk, this time. "I don't need one."

She knew, logically, that Tristan had to mean that whatever it was he did as a semi-secret agent, it didn't involve crazy shootouts and car chases like a spy movie. But she remembered the way he had just stood there and made Daniel back down, his unmovable cool confidence.

No, I'll bet you don't need a gun at all.

Poppy closed his passport and slipped it back into the inside pocket in his jacket, curling closer to him again. For half a second she considered whether it should feel different now, being so cozy with someone with so many secrets, but she'd known from the first second she laid eyes on him that there had to be something under that cool exterior, something she wouldn't be able to guess. She still wouldn't have felt safer anywhere else in the world, and she still wanted to get closer to him than she dared in the back of a cab.

"I don't need to know your last name, or what you're doing here. I believe that you're telling me as much of the truth as you can, and you haven't lied to me."

"I don't want to lie to you," Tristan agreed, running his fingers over her hair. "I want to be worthy of your trust, Poppy."

Poppy had to close her eyes at that, curling close to him to avoid the serious steadiness of his gaze. She wanted to ask him whether secret-agenting left him time for girlfriends, but she wasn't going to bring that up in the back of the cab. She stayed there, breathing the clean scent of his shirt, feeling the occasional faint touch of his fingers on her hair, letting the cab carry them to wherever they were going.

She was halfway to dreaming, drifting on thoughts of lying with Tristan in a wide bed with clean-smelling sheets and a view of the sea, when he said, "Poppy?"

She picked her head up and blinked at the brightness of the lights. They had drawn up to the door of the hotel, and two uniformed men were waiting to help them with their bags and usher them inside.

Maybe a little bit James Bond, Poppy thought, but she just nodded and grabbed her pack while Tristan opened the door. Tristan handed her out of the cab, waving off the hovering hotel employee, and Poppy swung the pack up onto her shoulder automatically. As soon as she did she realized it would have been more proper to hand it to someone else to carry for her, but her hand tightened on the strap as she thought it. She could carry her own bag, and she wasn't letting go of it now.

Tristan just squeezed her hand and said, "Shall we get inside?"

Poppy nodded quickly.

Someone opened the door for them, and Poppy nodded vaguely toward him, wondering if she was supposed to tip, or thank him, or what. But Tristan towed her into the lobby without breaking stride, all marble and thick rugs and fine furniture.

"Ah, there he is," Tristan murmured. "I'm traveling with an... assistant. Your long-lost brother, there."

Poppy looked in the direction of Tristan's slight nod, quickly spotting the guy with bright red hair wearing a black suit like Tristan's. He was standing by a pillar, and his posture was perfect except that he had his head down over his phone. Tristan led her over to him.

"Peter."

Peter looked up, straightening to something like attention and all but hiding his phone behind his back, like Tristan might not notice. He was definitely not in Tristan's league when it came to poker faces.

Poppy bit her lip and glanced up at Tristan. His face was almost unreadable—definitely lacking any of the tiny smiles she'd seen tonight. She hoped she wasn't about to find out that Tristan was an asshole boss; that would put a damper on this whole thing.

"Making an interim report?" Tristan asked.

Peter's eyes darted to her as he flushed the painful, obvious pink that was the redhead's curse. Poppy felt her own cheeks heat a little in sympathy.

"Just... keeping up on ancillary developments," Peter said, fairly evenly, though he couldn't quite seem to meet Tristan's eyes. "Sorry, I... sorry. Is this...?"

"Yes," Tristan said, allowing Peter to change the subject and at least not saying anything mean. "This young lady is named Poppy. I met her earlier and separated her from a disagreeable gentleman, and we agreed that she would be safer sharing my accommodations tonight. Shall we go up?"

Peter frowned a little, like that wasn't quite what he had expected to hear. He didn't seem totally shocked by Tristan's behavior, but he was still thrown off. "I... see. Yes. I have the keys—adjoining rooms."

Tristan nodded and turned, guiding Poppy toward the

elevators as Peter followed. None of them spoke in the elevator, but Poppy watched the way Peter kept looking at Tristan, then quickly away. He didn't look at her at all, but she had a feeling that that was because he was being careful not to.

When they reached their floor, Peter said nothing but the room number, gesturing down the hall. When they reached it he handed Tristan a keycard, nodding at the neighboring door. "That's mine. Your bags are in yours already."

Tristan handed the keycard over to Poppy. "You can lock the adjoining door on your side, so that I have to knock. If you want to take a shower or make any calls, feel free. I need to catch up with Peter. All right?"

Poppy glanced between them and then nodded agreement. Poppy was glad to see that he looked more curious than nervous about talking to Tristan. Poppy accepted the keycard and let herself into the room while the two men stood behind her.

She leaned against the hallway door to close it faster and set the chain on the door while she listened to the faint sounds of Tristan and Peter going into the room next door. Then she went to the adjoining door and *un*locked it.

She *did* want a shower, though, and she ought to finally take off Tristan's suit coat.

She laid it out on the room's one king-sized bed, and carefully turned the sleeves back down, brushing a hand over the hint of a crease in the heavy fabric. She thought about bringing it into the bathroom for the steam, then she shook her head—this was definitely the kind of hotel that would press Tristan's suit for him if he needed it. She picked up her pack, carrying it into the bathroom.

She shut and locked that door behind her, and just stood for a moment looking at herself in the wide mirror. She was still looking pale, which might have been the lighting in this opulent bathroom, though she had a feeling it was designed to be flattering to its normal wealthy occupants. She looked small, and wide-eyed, and alone, and like she'd reached the end of an unreasonably long night.

Poppy shook her head and stripped off her dress, bra, and panties, piling them on the counter. She dug into her pack for clean underwear and a t-shirt and yoga pants for pajamas. She pictured, for a second, stepping out of the bathroom in nothing but a posh hotel robe, letting it fall open while Tristan watched...

It sounded like it would be fun, some other time—she felt a little tingle run through her at the thought of Tristan's amber eyes heating as they traced over her body, looking at her everywhere with that same serious gaze—but mostly she was tired, and longing to be clean.

Shower, right, that was why she had come in here. She figured out the taps quickly enough, then sniffed the fancy complimentary soaps and shampoos. They were a pleasing, if slightly bewildering, mix of green tea and lavender; good enough for Poppy. She stepped under the hot water and just stood for a moment, letting her exhaustion catch up with her.

She'd only just arrived in London today, after five precarious days of travel—planes, trains, automobiles, a godawful amount of walking—from Melbourne, and that was before Sasha, Daniel, and all of that drama. She rubbed at her arm where Daniel had been gripping it, when he decided it was time for Poppy to come back to his place with him.

Daniel had *definitely* expected something. Poppy had absolutely no doubt of what he'd been expecting. What he still expected, because he was still convinced that Poppy was coming to Paris with him in the morning.

Bright and early, poppet. It wasn't hard to imagine an *or else* on the end of that.

But she was safe here. Tristan wouldn't let anything happen to her, and this kind of hotel wouldn't let Daniel in the door. She was safe, and Sasha was safe, and Tristan was waiting for her just outside.

Poppy half-dried her hair, brushed her teeth, and, after a second of considering the bathrobe and some sexy come-on routine, pulled on her own pajamas. Tristan was getting her the way she was—no point trying to fool a secret agent into thinking she was the fancy-negligee type.

When she opened the door, the first thing she saw was Tristan hanging up his suit coat. She stayed right there in the doorway as he took off his tie and looped it around the top of the hanger.

He turned toward her as he unbuttoned the collar of his shirt, his eyes finding her as if he had known exactly where she was. She waited for his eyes to skim lower, for him to remark on what she was wearing, but he didn't. He held her gaze, and she realized that he always had, even that first second when their eyes met.

She thought that he wasn't looking in the same way that Peter hadn't looked at her in the elevator: because he was being very careful not to look. Not because he didn't want to see.

"I hope you don't mind," Poppy said, stepping out of the doorway and gesturing down at her pajamas to see if he would follow the gesture with his eyes. "My wardrobe runs pretty casual."

Tristan unbuttoned another button of his shirt, revealing more warm brown skin, the hollow between his collarbones and the top of his chest. He was walking toward her slowly as he said, "Wear anything you like, Poppy. I promise you, it makes no difference to me."

Poppy swallowed and stood her ground as Tristan came closer, until he was close enough to touch. In her bare feet and pajamas, she was even more conscious of how much taller he was. When he was close enough to kiss, she still couldn't reach, but she could feel the warmth of him, his closeness making her whole body wake up. Her breasts tingled, and she couldn't help being aware that they were only covered by a thin, worn t-shirt.

Tristan put his hand on her shoulder and bent just far enough to press his lips to her forehead.

"You're perfect in anything," he murmured, and as he stepped past her and into the bathroom he added, so low she might have imagined it, "Or in nothing."

Poppy turned on her heel, but the bathroom door closed firmly behind him. She stared for a moment, wondering what to make of that, and then she walked over to the enormous bed and peeled back the covers, planting herself firmly in the middle.

5

POPPY

Poppy hadn't meant to fall asleep, but it had been a terribly long day, and the hotel was so quiet, the pillows so incredibly soft.

She didn't know how long she had been when she opened her eyes to low light and Tristan lying on the edge of the bed facing her. She was all the way under the covers and he lay on top of them, so she could see that he'd stripped down to boxers and an undershirt, leaving acres of brown skin and muscular body on display. She was suddenly wide awake, her body flushing hot as she got wet between her legs.

It wasn't her most graceful moment, but Poppy didn't waste any time about shoving the blankets down and scooting across the ridiculously wide bed to kiss him.

Tristan's arm went around her instantly, and he let out a shaky breath against her mouth like he'd been holding it, or had been in pain and now was relieved. Poppy made a soft soothing noise and kissed him again and again, little brushes of lips, until Tristan's arm around her tightened and he rolled her onto her back, bracing himself above her as he took charge of the kissing.

Her mouth opened instinctively to his, and his tongue pressed in, exploring her, taking thorough possession. Poppy moaned a little, *yes, please*, but that made Tristan draw back, which wasn't what she had wanted at all.

"Hello," he said softly, not silly or teasing. Like it mattered that he greet her properly before they went further than those few kisses.

"Hi," Poppy said, raising her hands from where she was instinctively clutching at his shirt. She hooked one behind his neck and tucked the other behind her head. "Why aren't you kissing me anymore?"

Tristan sighed again, but he did kiss her some more. Just little pecks now, more promises of kisses than proper kisses themselves. In between he spoke a few words at a time. "Because I—was going—to take things—slow—and not—scare you off."

"I'm not scared," Poppy promised him, but as soon as the words were out of her mouth she was wondering if she should be.

This whole night had been insane, from rescuing Sasha from Daniel's evil schemes to Tristan rescuing her from Daniel and turning out to be a secret agent. From *Denmark*. Who even knew Denmark had secret agents?

Her own reaction had been mostly submerged under freaking out when she first met him, but this attraction—the way she *trusted* him so instantaneously—was nothing Poppy had ever felt before. She had met her share of hot guys, and good ones, and she had gone to bed a time or two with guys she didn't know as well as she should have. But Tristan was different. This all felt different.

Tristan seemed to sense her second-guessing. He kissed her, very softly, one last time. Then he sat up, gently pushing Poppy away.

She scooted back as she sat up to face him, curling up in the drift of fluffy pillows against the padded headboard.

"It's all right to be scared," Tristan said, sitting cross-legged with his hands on his knees, so that she had an unobstructed view of his blue-and-white striped boxers and the round bulge of his half-hard cock behind them.

Poppy belatedly dragged her gaze up to his face, and found him looking at her with a slight smile, not amused at her but... encouraging, maybe.

Poppy smiled back. "I'm not *that* scared. Just a little nervous, maybe."

Tristan unfolded one leg, nudging her foot with his toes. "What do you need to be nervous about? It's just me and you, and I swear that I am only interested in what you're interested in."

Poppy turned her foot, wriggling her toes against his like they could hold feet instead of holding hands. She had exactly enough time to think that she shouldn't let him see her toes, and then realized that his were as knobbly with calluses and possible old breaks as her own. She leaned forward, cupping her hand around his foot and looking at it, and saw the familiar wonky toenails and small scars.

She looked up at him with a smile. "Went barefoot a lot as a kid?"

He winced a little, like maybe it wasn't a good memory, but before she could apologize his expression settled back to his usual seriousness. "Constantly. And it's all rocks, where I grew up—when it's not snow and ice."

Tristan leaned in enough to curl his hand reciprocally around her foot, thumb brushing gently over a fresher scar. "Not just when you were a kid, I see?"

"Doesn't matter how much my mom insisted my feet would toughen up if I went barefoot," Poppy agreed, shaking her head. She really should've thought to wear sandals that day. "Sharp rocks are still sharp."

Tristan leaned in and kissed her, a little off-center on her mouth, splitting the difference between kissing her on the cheek and on the lips. He sat back, putting both hands down on the bed as he did, but he left his foot pressed close to hers.

Poppy mirrored him, leaning back against the headboard. "Taking it slow, huh?"

Tristan smiled one of his barely-visible smiles, a corner of his mouth turning up. "Trying to. I fear I'm not very good at it."

"I bet you are, usually," Poppy said. "I bet you usually have everything under control, don't do one thing you didn't think through. I'm the one who never walks when I can run."

"I invited you to my hotel room," Tristan pointed out.

"I dared you to share the bed," Poppy returned. "You're the kind of guy who totally would have slept on the floor or in the other room if I hadn't made it pretty clear I wanted you here."

Something hot and dark flashed through Tristan's eyes, and he looked down as he said, "Don't ever doubt that I want to be here, Poppy. I know am not... expressive, but. Please don't doubt that."

Poppy swallowed hard, feeling an answering heat flare in her body, mingled strangely with the urge to pull Tristan into her arms and promise that she would never think badly of him just because he wasn't all smiles and flirty talk.

"Anyway," she said, keeping still with an effort. She wasn't going to rush him. "What I really meant is... if you meant to take it slow, then you meant to... to stick around for a while."

Tristan looked up at that and met her eyes. "Yes. As long as it takes."

Poppy's heart beat faster, and she squirmed under his intense look, pressing her thighs together and rocking her hips irresistibly. "You don't do anything without being really, really serious about it, do you?"

Tristan smiled, showing his teeth for the first time. It looked a little predatory, and she couldn't decide if it looked like he was out practice at smiling or if that was just exactly how he felt. "I don't."

Poppy bit her lip. "I'm not... not good at sticking with things for the long haul. Always on the move."

Tristan's smile vanished into blankness so fast she almost thought she'd imagined it. "I had guessed that."

Poppy raised her eyebrows, fighting not to laugh. Sherlock Holmes, incoming. "How could you tell?"

Tristan tilted his head. "American in London with no particular responsibilities but without the attitude to suggest that you expect your family, or your family's money, to solve any problem you run into. Staying in a hostel and carrying what looks like everything you own in a well-traveled pack. And you weren't at all impressed by my measly few passport stamps."

Poppy laughed, clapping her hand over her mouth as she did. She didn't want to insult him, but it was true, of course. She probably had ten times as many stamps as Tristan did, almost all of them acquired in just over a year.

Tristan shook his head a little, but his smile faded quickly, and Poppy had no desire to laugh at his seriousness.

"Is that how you prefer things?" He asked quietly. "Changing all the time, never staying with one..."

Poppy shook her head hard before she could summon the words. "I think I... I just don't know how. Or I just never had anybody else who would stay in one place for me. With me."

Tristan said nothing, just watching her with his serious gaze that defied the amber-brightness of his eyes.

"You would, though, wouldn't you?" Poppy said, unable to look away. "If I told you I needed a week, or a month, or—or a year. You would wait, and when I came back to find you, you would be right here."

"I wouldn't be able to resist following you, if you made me wait a whole year," Tristan said. "But I wouldn't press you, or try to make you change your mind. I would just... need to see you, now and then. Hear your voice, catch your scent in the air."

Logically, Poppy knew that that translated to *I would definitely stalk you if you left me*, but she couldn't feel any fear, even then. She knew what Tristan was saying, and what he wasn't. *I would follow you to the end of the earth. I would be there for you if you needed me, wherever there might be.*

But still he was keeping his distance, demanding nothing. Keeping himself under control.

"Why don't you come and catch my scent right here, then," Poppy said, crooking one finger as she spoke.

She saw the muscle work in Tristan's jaw when he looked away. It was costing him some effort to restrain himself, to take it slow, to be careful and responsible.

Poppy wasn't having any of that. She reached down and tugged her loose t-shirt up. She barely had it off, her hands over her head and wrists crossed, when Tristan was right there, leaning over her and kissing her.

One of his hands curled gently around her wrists, pressing them to the padded headboard, and she knew that as soft as his grip might seem, she wouldn't be able to break it if she tried.

His mouth was hot and demanding on hers, and Poppy opened to him without hesitation, her legs parting at the same time so that he could move closer between them. His free hand found her breast, cupping it and stroking his thumb over her nipple, and Poppy moaned against his lips as he licked into her. She squirmed under him, feeling the strength of his body over her as he held her there, kissing her thoroughly and teasing her breasts.

When he let up so she could breathe, Poppy only had time to gasp before he was kissing her again, his hand roaming over her body everywhere except where she wanted it the most. She curled her legs up until her feet were at his waist, and she got one toe into the waistband of his boxers and started trying to push them down.

Tristan pulled back to suck in a breath. He squeezed his hand around her wrists as his other hand cupped her breast again. "Let me, Poppy."

"Not if you're going to *take it slow*," Poppy insisted, even though she was still panting herself.

Tristan kissed her again, so hard her lips felt bruised and she couldn't think of anything past the heat of his mouth claiming hers, his body close but just out of reach.

"I'm not taking *it*," he murmured in her ear, his voice so low and rough it was nearly a growl, sending shivers down her spine and making her hotter and wetter than ever at her core. "I'm taking *you*, and I'm going to take you right."

Poppy moaned at that, wrapping her legs around his waist and arching toward him, wordlessly begging for him to take as much of her as he wanted, *now*. Tristan rocked a little, letting her get the barest touch of his hardness through her pants and his boxers. As soon as she felt it she knew she needed him inside her, pulses of wet heat surging between her thighs, but Tristan kept on kissing and teasing until she was whimpering with need.

Just when she thought she couldn't take it anymore, Tristan drew back from kissing to pull her down the bed, laying her flat on her back with her wrists pressed to the mattress above her head.

"Are you going to be still," Tristan growled, "or do I have to keep holding you here?"

Poppy felt like her brain melted a little from the heat in his voice, and she nodded as she moaned.

Tristan showed his teeth. "That wasn't a yes or no question, my—Poppy. But I think I know what you mean."

"Please," Poppy managed. That wasn't an answer either, but Tristan didn't argue, just started kissing his way down her throat. Both of his hands settled over her breasts, covering them completely and drawing more pleasure from the touch than she had ever felt before.

"Yes," she gasped, as his mouth followed his hands, his tongue flicking at one hard nipple. "Yes, Tristan, *please*."

Tristan's hands slid down, fingers tucking into the top

of her yoga pants, and Poppy tried to wriggle helpfully, only to have her hips pressed down firmly into the mattress. Her eyes flashed open at the show of strength, and she moaned, squirming more just to feel how he held her there, firmly but without hurting her at all.

She knew, distantly, that if she could just hold still he would do what she wanted, but she needed him too much, needed to *do* something. Her hands were clutching the pillows, trying to keep still, but she couldn't make her body stop moving, seeking more of his touch.

"I can't," she gasped. "Tristan, please, I can't, I can't stop."

He moved immediately, his hands coming up to frame her face as he kissed her, his hips settling between her thighs as he rocked against her, holding her pinned in place. Now she could feel how hard he was, and knew that he needed her just as much as she needed him, no matter how he was trying to do this right.

His kisses were soft, almost soothing, a gentle contrast to their hips grinding together.

"All right," he whispered. "All right, Poppy. Maybe another time we'll go slow. When we don't need it so much."

"So like, thirty, forty years," Poppy gasped, and she saw the bright flash of Tristan's teeth before he was moving again, moving down her body as he tugged her yoga pants off.

She'd already forgotten what she had said when Tristan murmured, "I'll put it on the calendar," and then her pants were all the way off, and Tristan was kneeling between her thighs. As he looked down at her, Poppy abruptly found out that she could hold perfectly still after all.

She hadn't exactly planned on this; she really hadn't done this much at all, especially not this spontaneously. Her thighs were covered with fine faint down where she hadn't bothered shaving all the way up, and the puff of dark red curls between her legs was decidedly untamed.

"Red all over, huh," Tristan murmured, looking up at her, and Poppy groaned as she remembered her flippant remark. She felt the heat in her skin flaring hotter, and knew that she was flushing a brighter pink from her forehead to her chest.

"It's beautiful."

Poppy gasped and opened her eyes at a light, delicate touch between her legs.

"You're beautiful." Tristan's fingers stroked the outer lips of her, damp and sensitive with need. "Lovely. Just as you are. Just Poppy."

Poppy spread her legs wider, begging without words, and his fingertips dipped further in, finding her wet hot core and teasing the opening there. Even his fingers would be bigger than anything she'd had inside her lately, and Poppy was ready, panting for it. When he did press inside, slowly and gently, his touch was everything she had needed, a delicious hot stretch that made her moan and lift her hips for more.

"Yes," she gasped, "Tristan—"

She reached for him, sinking her fingers into the silky black curls of his hair, and he moved up to kiss her again, his fingers stroking deeper and deeper inside her. His thumb circled over her mound, giving her just the right pressure to push up against as he drove her wild, and his kisses were quick and sweet.

The pleasure built and built, and Tristan kept up a relentless pace, never letting her catch her breath. She was gasping and clinging to him when the storm of sensation broke over her, and she cried out again and again as her climax overwhelmed her senses.

When she finally came down from it, Tristan slipped his fingers free, resting his hand on her hip as he kissed her more deeply. She let that go on for a little while, then pushed him back. Her arms were like noodles, but Tristan let himself be moved, propping himself over her on one arm.

"How are you still wearing *clothes*?" Poppy demanded. "Come on, it's your turn."

"Not very many clothes," Tristan pointed out, but he sat up when she gave him another floppy-armed nudge. "But, as you are so impatient, of course."

Poppy folded her arms behind her head at that, trying to sprawl languidly instead of looking like she was still trying to remember how her muscles worked. Tristan peeled out of his shirt and shoved down his boxers, and stayed sitting beside her for a moment, letting her look her fill.

He was gorgeous from head to toe, tall and lean with obvious strength in every inch of his body. His brown skin gleamed in the low, golden light, and his amber eyes gleamed. His erection jutted up against his belly, darker than the rest of his skin, beautiful and thick with desire— all for her.

"Come here," Poppy said, keeping her arms folded behind her head, her legs spread where she was wet and sensitive and already hungry for more. For *him*. "I don't think you've taken nearly enough of me yet."

"Well," he murmured, moving to brace himself over her, one hand stroking over the swell of her hip. "I shall have to rectify that, hm?"

Poppy nodded, reaching up to curl one hand around his neck. He leaned down for another kiss, and another, his body settling lower over hers until she could feel the hard length of him against her belly. She tried to squirm up under him, to get them lined up properly, but Tristan moved every time she did, so they were migrating across the bed without Poppy ever getting Tristan quite where she wanted him. She would have argued, but she couldn't quite stop kissing him, and the feeling of his body braced above hers, all that strength held so carefully in check, was a pleasure of its own.

Then Tristan moved above her, reaching for something. Poppy turned her head to see what it was, and

Tristan held up a little foil square between two fingers. "Would you like to help move things along, or hold still and watch?"

Poppy reached for his hand at the same time it occurred to her that her experience getting condoms onto men she found this maddeningly attractive was... nonexistent. She let her hand fall against the pillow.

"I'll watch."

Tristan smiled widely and gave her a quick, soft kiss. "Be still and don't distract me, then."

Poppy stuck her tongue out, but she flung her other hand out and let her legs flop on the bed. Tristan got up on his knees and tore the condom packet open, and Poppy couldn't look at anything but his erection as he stroked it, first with his bare hand, then rolling down the condom over it. As soon as it was in place, she wriggled, tilting her hips up and lifting her knees.

Tristan shook his head with a stern look that she knew was teasing even as it sent a hot little thrill down her spine. He lowered himself over her again, his fingers slipping between her thighs to press inside. Poppy let her eyes close as he stroked her, and she felt herself getting wetter again, ready to welcome him.

Then Tristan's fingers withdrew, and she felt the blunt, hot pressure of him pressing inside her. She gasped, and Tristan was there, kissing her cheek, nuzzling at her temple, and all the time pushing deeper into her, filling her up so exquisitely.

"Oh, oh, *Tristan*," Poppy gasped. It all felt new, as if she'd never done this the way she was with him, as if it was something different, something *more*, with this man. "That's so good, you're so—"

He covered her mouth with his, kissing her quiet as he moved fully inside her. He was still for a moment, and she tipped her head back to breathe, adjusting to the feeling of him so deep within her. She bit her lip, holding back all the things it was way too soon to say, no matter how serious

Tristan was, no matter how much she wanted it to be true.

"My Poppy," Tristan murmured, when she couldn't say anything at all. He kissed her gently, again and again, as he started to move. "You feel like you were made for me. Is it the same for you?"

His accent was heavier, she noticed, and she smiled up at him and wondered if she could drive him to forget to speak English altogether. She rolled her hips, moaning as she did it for the delicious feel of him moving inside her, touching every secret sweet spot.

"Tell me," he whispered in her ear. "Is it good for you, my Poppy? My sweet?"

"Better than good." Poppy moved again, knowing that it wouldn't be long before Tristan took over again. "*Best*. Best ever. It's never been like this before."

"Of course not." Tristan's hand tightened on her hip, tilting her to a slightly different angle, and then he started to move. Poppy was quickly lost in bliss, but she didn't miss the fact that Tristan started speaking some other language right around then, sweet-sounding words she couldn't understand. But the sound of his voice told her everything she needed to know, and as he picked up speed his voice deepened into a growl again.

Poppy put her hands above her head, clutching the pillow and surrendering herself utterly to her lover. Tristan really growled at that, a wordless sound that vibrated through her whole body as he thrust inside her, finding just the right angle to set off fireworks through her whole body.

She had no idea how long it went on, the pleasure turning her whole body molten and her mind a whirl of sensation. Tristan kept asking her something in his language that she didn't understand, and she cried out a wordless answer that felt like the truth. He kissed her hard, then, thrusting deep inside her, and she tipped over the edge into another climax.

This one seemed to go on and on with Tristan still

moving within her, until he went still and quiet, and she felt the throbbing of his hardness inside her as he came. She lay gasping for a while, letting her brain reassemble itself. Her body felt like it was lit up from the inside, like amber shining in sunlight.

Tristan shifted away from her, just enough to turn off the light, and then curled himself around her, tucking her close to the warmth of his naked body. They could still strike sparks, she thought, half-tempted to go again, even though the darkness and her exhaustion was dragging her under. Even tired as she was she could feel a certain unsatisfied desire thrumming between them. Once hadn't been enough. There wouldn't ever be enough.

She never wanted to leave this spot. She never wanted to go anywhere else at all. When she heard the faint, distant buzz of her phone, she snuggled into Tristan's arms, telling herself, *I'll look at it in the morning.*

6

POPPY

Poppy woke up already out of bed and headed for the bathroom. She stopped, looking around in the not-quite-complete darkness, because there was too much *room* around her; for a moment she couldn't hear anyone else nearby at all, and then she looked back toward the bed and saw Tristan lying there.

He pushed up on one elbow and she grinned, remembering—not-exactly-secret agent, posh hotel—and shook her head at him, gesturing toward the bathroom. He nodded, and she had the sense of a smile in it though it was too dark to read his barely-there expressions. But the sooner she got on with what she'd gotten up for, the sooner she could be back in bed with him.

She hurried into the bathroom, shutting the door before she considered the light switches. Then she remembered that her phone was on the bathroom counter, and she hit the button to light that up instead, creating enough glow so she could do what she'd come in for.

That meant her text notifications were all visible on the screen while she was washing her hands, and she couldn't help reading them; there were enough from Daniel to fill the screen, and just one from Sasha: *wtf how does he remember the town where my aunt lives???*

Poppy felt cold. If Daniel went after Sasha, or her aunt... She scrolled through the rest of the texts, all smarmy promises and thinly-veiled threats about how she didn't want to miss this trip with him. *Bright and early, or else.*

It was going on five now. He didn't expect her to meet him until half-past six. There was time to... to what? She wasn't going anywhere with him, wasn't doing him any favors—not in an airport, where she risked getting grabbed by security and disappeared into terrorist-detention if she figured out what he was doing and tried to tell them.

But if it was something like that, she *had* to try to stop him. If there was a chance of people getting hurt, maybe killed, and she heard about it on the news and realized she could have stopped it and instead she'd gone back to bed with Tristan...

She had to do something, but right now she didn't know enough to do anything useful. So she had to find out what the hell Daniel was planning.

There was always a plan at the back of her mind for how to leave wherever she was: take the most important things, leave anything that might slow her down. She could be at the nearest Tube station in five minutes, and her pack was right here in the bathroom. She was getting dressed before she thought about anything else, and then she started pulling the most important stuff out of her bulky hiking pack.

Her passport and enough cash for transit in small bills and coins, that was in an inside zippered pocket. The plastic in-case-of-emergency bag with contact information, the handful of actual photos she kept with her, and her own real phone, the one she'd turned off a couple of days ago so she could have some time to herself. Wrapped up in her fleece, her few pieces of jewelry and other little mementos that she really cared about, her stuffed bunny, and her backup cash. Her good boots.

She stopped then, looking down at the stuff she'd pulled out and thinking about what she was about to do. If she was going *toward* danger... She had to leave most of this stuff here. If something went terribly wrong while she was trying to figure out what was going on with Daniel, she wanted most of this stuff as far away from her as she could get it.

And this hotel, with Tristan, this was the safest place she knew right now.

She dug into her pack again, pulling out a different assortment of stuff—dress, raincoat, shoulder bag, some random stuff that would look like she might genuinely have packed for a short trip. Nothing special, nothing she cared about. She couldn't avoid taking her passport and some cash, but she left behind her other ID, including the tattered photocopy of her passport, and everything else with any value.

That had only lost her ten minutes. She could still get to the airport before Daniel would expect her to be there. Watch for him, figure out what his plan was before he spotted her, and then, when she had something she could actually tell security or the police or someone... then she could do something about it. Before he did anything to Sasha, or anyone else.

She just had to get out of the hotel room, first. She tucked the phone she'd been using into her raincoat pocket and slung her bag on her shoulder, picked up the pair of sandals she would wear, and slipped out quietly into the room.

She didn't let herself look toward the bed. Tristan would wake up or he wouldn't, and she didn't have time to hesitate.

Her hand was on the door handle when she heard a sharp movement behind her and looked back. Tristan was sitting bolt upright in the bed, and her eyes had adjusted enough to see that his eyes were wide.

"Go back to sleep," she said, low but not whispering. "I just have to go do something, and then I'll be back."

"Poppy," Tristan's voice was very calm, as though nothing about this situation surprised him. "Don't do this. I can protect you from him."

Poppy couldn't help a little smile, her heart beating faster at the way he obviously, instantly understood. But she had to do this, and she didn't want to drag Tristan into whatever this was when she didn't know anything for sure. It might be nothing, and it might be something horrific, and she needed to know that what she left behind here—not just her things, but this man—would be safe, waiting for her right where she left them, so she could come back.

"I know." She sounded almost as calm as Tristan, somehow. It helped, knowing there was somewhere to come back to, someone who would wait. "But being safe isn't the only thing that matters, is it? You're a secret agent, you know that. And I won't be in danger, really. Give me a couple of hours and I'll be back, safe and sound."

"Let me help," Tristan offered after a pause. "Even a secret agent doesn't go into a mission without backup."

She shook her head. "It has to be me, and I have to be alone, Tris. I'll be okay. I'll be back soon."

She had to believe that part. She had to believe there was something to come back to.

"Tell me," Tristan started, but Poppy shook her head.

"No time. I'll be back, I swear. I'm not running. It's just something I have to do. Please, just—wait for me, okay?"

Tristan moved like he was going to get out of bed, and Poppy knew she couldn't drag this out any longer. Even if she could possibly explain it to him, just waiting for him to get dressed was more time than she could spare.

Poppy shook her head, blew him a kiss, and then darted out the door.

ROYAL GUARD TIGER

~~*

Halfway to Heathrow, Poppy transformed herself into someone Daniel would never recognize. It didn't take much—men like Daniel didn't look closely. To him Poppy was *red hair, lots of pale skin showing, giggly, dancing girl.*

She went heavy on bronzer and then covered her hair in a black scarf, wrapping it closely around her throat and tucking it into the collar of her raincoat, which she buttoned right up to her throat. She unbelted the raincoat, folding up the belt and tucking it into one pocket where she could reach it easily. The dress she'd pulled on was dark blue and brushed the tops of her feet, and her raincoat fell to her shins—one advantage of being short. She darkened her brows and did her lips in a dramatic shade that would have clashed with her hair if it was showing, slipped on a pair of big dark sunglasses, and *voila*, she was invisible to Daniel: someone he would never bother to hit on and therefore a woman his eyes would pass right over.

She got a coffee and texted Daniel as she scouted for a good spot near the doors into the International Departures area. *Just leaving, so excited! Where should I meet you? Xx*

Daniel texted her back almost instantly with—well, a lot of nastiness that she took to mean she was making him nervous, and then a door number.

Poppy went over to the next door down from that one and sipped her coffee, periodically holding her phone to her ear and snapping out angry questions about *where are you?* And, *My mother's surgery will not wait for your breakfast! I will get on that plane without you!* in heavily accented French.

It was only a few minutes before Daniel got out of a car, pulling one discreet black carry-on and carrying one ostentatiously pink gift bag with a cheap bouquet stuck in the top.

Then three more guys got out of the car, which Poppy got a picture of while grumbling at her phone like she was checking her flight's status. The three guys all looked about as big and mean as Daniel, but none of them were carrying luggage. They spread out without Daniel giving them instructions; one walked right past Poppy to enter through the door she was standing by.

Daniel, meanwhile, pulled out his phone to text her again. He kept his own carry-on bag between his feet while he did, but he never let go of the gift bag at all, even though it was big enough to be kind of unwieldy. He kept it tucked close against his body, even crumpling it a little, as he texted her.

Not a bomb, Poppy thought. He wouldn't clutch a bomb like that—and of course it wouldn't be a bomb, really. Now that she wasn't panicking in a dark bathroom that seemed kind of obvious; Daniel was into whatever he was into for profit, and to feel like a big bad guy. Some kind of airport attack wouldn't do that for him.

And it meant that there was some object in the bag that was important, vital. He wanted Poppy to smuggle something, then, maybe drugs, maybe something stolen. So it wasn't about getting Poppy—or Sasha, or any woman—to go somewhere with him. He just needed someone who looked less suspicious than he did to get whatever was in that bag through airport security.

And he had three guys watching to make sure it went right, which meant that Poppy couldn't just waltz up to him and ask what was in the bag and then take off. She remembered his grip on her arm and thought that she really, really didn't want to get within grabbing distance of him anyway.

She still didn't know what was in the bag, though. And she still really didn't want to let him get away with whatever he was planning—even if he didn't manage to get at Sasha as a Plan B or just to punish her and Poppy for messing up his plan, he didn't *deserve* to have this go well. She was right here, after all, there had to be *something* she could do to ruin his day without ruining her own ten times worse.

Poppy lifted her phone to her ear and repeated her well-worn, *Where are you? You're supposed to be here by now!* in French.

Right behind her, Tristan said softly, "I'm here, of course."

7

TRISTAN

After making love to his mate for the first time—after telling her how he felt about her, if thankfully in Valtyran so that she didn't run screaming away from him—Tristan had felt truly content for the first time in a very long time.

Lying there, holding Poppy, let himself drift into dreams of their future together. He would show her the beauty and wonder of Valtyra—reunite her with her family. Further on, he was standing on the edge of a mountain lake and watching Poppy wade into the water holding a tan-skinned toddler by the hand, the child's dark auburn curls hiding their face.

He wanted to walk closer, to lift his child into his arms and see the color of their eyes, see their smile, but he didn't give in to the impulse. He stayed still, watching at a little distance. Instead of feeling furious with himself for failing to reach out, he thought, *No, best to leave a few surprises.*

He realized he was dreaming then, and opened his eyes to find that Poppy was indeed out of his reach; the sound of waves was the sound of the bathroom fan running. He lay drowsily still, watching the line of light and thinking how strange, how wonderful, it was that his body already knew and trusted his mate so well that he had not been wakened by her slipping out of bed.

But she had not come back to bed. When she stood there with her hand on the door and told him she had to go, that she had to do something alone, he had been unable to make her understand that he couldn't let her go. His tiger had roared and raged within him at the thought of his mate in danger, unprotected, but Tristan himself had just sat there, calm and quiet, never raising his voice, never telling her how he felt about any of it.

When the door closed and he was alone, at least he could *move*. Tristan rushed into motion, pounding on the door to wake Peter as he yanked on his clothes. All the time he had been aware of the feeling of Poppy getting further away—his tiger had her scent now, and he knew the sound of her beating heart better than his own mother's voice. He could track her anywhere, even in this crowded place.

He would not lose her again, even if he had been unable to break through his own control to make her stay.

Still, there was no way he was going to let her down. He was only a handful of minutes behind her when he rushed out of the hotel. I wasn't hard to guess, between his sense of her and the logic of the situation, that she would have gone straight for the Underground station. It was more or less directly across the street from the hotel.

The Kingdom of Denmark had its embassy only a few blocks up the street, and Tristan was on the phone to their designated liaison with the Kingdom of Valtyra while he was hurrying down to the train platform. Poppy would be headed toward Heathrow, of course. She hadn't denied it when he implied she was going to meet Daniel, and he had wanted to take her on some trip this morning, "bright and early." This train would take her straight to the airport, and Tristan was going with her.

The train arrived before he found her in the crowd on the platform, so he boarded near the back. His sense of her was still *too far away*, but she didn't seem to move any further away while they were on the train, so Tristan occupied himself with making sure he looked presentable and making sure that Peter and some backup from the Danish Embassy, with proper credentials to flash around at the airport, would be following him there.

He touched the pocket of his jacket that held his passport, and then the other pocket—which held a Danish passport for Poppy, indicating her diplomatic immunity. If things got really bad, he could bail her out of just about anything with that, and the officers from the embassy would back him.

If it came to that, the main problem would be explaining it all to Poppy, and he wouldn't have much choice but to haul her back to Valtyra, since no one in England was going to very pleased with either of them.

Poppy would be least pleased of all.

But she would understand, in time. She would forgive him. He would find a way to make her understand, to make things right with her. She was his mate, and he couldn't do less than everything. He would find some way to show her, prove to her, how he needed her, how he loved her.

I love her. For a few seconds Tristan just stared down at his hands and thought of it. *I love her. She is my mate, and we will be together, and even if she doesn't now, someday she will love me too.*

As long as I keep her safe and don't scare her worse than that scumbag.

Tristan found his lips twitching toward a smile; it was a little effort to make himself perfectly straight-faced again when he got off the train at the airport, once again following his sense of where Poppy was. It took him a moment to spot her, but by the time he saw her slim, lovely hands paying for her coffee, he knew she was the one in the long, loose coat and black headscarf. It was a good disguise; he could see the way people barely looked at her, and he knew Daniel would never look closely enough to recognize her.

Still, he recognized his mate in the way she moved, though her hair was covered and her slim shape was obscured. He would know her anywhere.

She obviously had some sort of plan that didn't involve going anywhere with Daniel, so Tristan hung back and watched the way people watched her and moved around her. He meant not to approach her until she seemed to have some need of him, but he could help drifting closer as he worked at blending in with the other passengers. He made a show of looking from monitors to his phone, not letting anyone see him take an interest in the woman with the headscarf who kept speaking French into her phone.

By the time he understood what she was saying, he was barely out of arm's reach of her. It was much closer than he had meant to come, and he knew he had to tell her he was there, if only to avoid spoiling her plans by startling her.

Besides, it was too good a line to resist. When she demanded, *Where are you?* Tristan answered her: "I'm here, of course."

For a second Poppy froze—not fear, he knew, but caution. He glanced around and realized that he could see Daniel waiting for her, holding a pink gift bag and standing careful guard over his own luggage.

Tristan's tiger growled a threat, but Tristan showed nothing, staying perfectly still.

Poppy tilted her head to her left, and Tristan murmured, "Of course," and turned to walk that way, keeping his eyes on an airport monitor. Poppy followed, coming to stand beside him in a spot where Daniel wouldn't be able to see from his position. Tristan didn't look over at her.

"He's got three accomplices, which is a little more than

I was expecting," Poppy murmured with no preamble. "One in the gray jacket on your left, eight o'clock."

Tristan glanced reflexively at the time before realizing that Poppy meant clock-face position. He glanced at the reflection in his phone screen until he'd identified the man.

"The other two I'm not sure where they are, they went the opposite direction. Pictures." Poppy held up her phone and thumbed quickly through a series of pictures: a car, Daniel and three big men getting out.

Tristan nodded. "Anything for me to do at all, Miss?"

He saw Poppy smile slightly in his peripheral vision. She slipped her sunglasses off, tucking them into her bag and withdrawing a small kit.

"Well, now that I've got my secret agent backup on the scene, I'm going to go tell Daniel to his face to go to hell." She took something from the little kit and wiped her face, returning her skin to its usual paleness, her lips to their natural pink. "If he tries to drag me to a plane, do you suppose you could get him arrested for assaulting me?"

"I would like nothing better," Tristan said, still watching in fascination as she applied different makeup to replace what she'd removed, lining her eyes and glossing her lips. "Although I don't think I could let him lay a hand on you."

"Well," Poppy said, smiling wider as she examined herself in the mirror. She tilted it so that their eyes met in the reflection, and her tone turning to one generously dispensing a treat. "That seems fine. Then *you* can press the charges, right?"

Tristan nodded, and tore his gaze from Poppy's reflection to alert the Danish attaché to his exact location and the likelihood of his becoming entangled in a— possibly quite extensive—fistfight in the next few minutes. Then he looked around for Peter, and found him standing perhaps fifty yards away, watching intently.

Peter gave him a firm nod. Tristan had no doubt he would have been able to hear Tristan and Poppy's conversation from there, with a shifter's senses all attuned to them. Tristan nodded back; he knew he should have conveyed confidence somehow, to let Peter know that he trusted him. He ought to have been able to express it, to reassure Peter that they both knew this wouldn't be like the last time they were both involved in a brawl.

Even as this distance, Tristan thought he saw Pete's gaze flick to the scars Peter's claws had left.

But this would be different, whether Tristan knew how to show it or not. As long as everyone, including Tristan, had judged Peter right, he would behave differently this time, even if Tristan was stone-faced as ever about it.

Then there was no more time to think or plan.

Poppy tugged the black scarf from where it covered her hair, folding it neatly before she tucked it into her bag. Without saying more, she turned away.

Tristan turned on his heel to follow, several steps behind. He stopped once he was near enough to see Daniel. Poppy had her raincoat off and folded it over one arm, waving to Daniel in a big, ostentatious gesture with the other.

"There you are!" She called out. "I've been looking and looking for you!"

"This is where I *told you* to meet me," Daniel snapped, moving toward her in long strides. "Come on, let's get to security, the flight's leaving soon."

"Hmm," Poppy said, moving gracefully to stay out of his reach. "Where are we going, exactly? Where's my boarding pass? I'll need that before I can go through security."

"I told you where we're going," Daniel said sharply, trying to herd her further inside. "Come on, we're going to be cutting it bloody close as it is."

"I want my present first," Poppy said, standing her ground. "I mean, I assume that's for me, it's not really your color."

"You can have your present when you've earned it,"

Daniel snapped, keeping a firm grip on the pink bag. "Now come *on*, we need to get in line for security."

"Not without my boarding pass I don't," Poppy repeated. "And definitely not until I know where you're planning to take me, and why."

Daniel's hand shot out, Poppy jerked back a half-step, and Tristan, moving faster than either of them, stepped in between his mate and the man who would dare to touch her against her will. He caught Daniel's wrist in a hard grip and held it immobile. Just that. Nothing more, though his tiger roared for it.

Daniel looked startled for a second, and then his features twisted in a sneer. "*You* again. What the fuck do you think you're—"

He looked past Tristan to Poppy as some degree of understanding dawned. "You lying little—"

Tristan adjusted his grip, tightening his hold and twisting just a little, enough to stop Daniel from saying something Tristan would be happy to make him regret. He saw Daniel register the pain, and Tristan's strength, and there was a flicker of some recognition in his eyes.

"*You.*" And then Daniel seemed to go berserk, lunging in at Tristan with a howl of rage, the arm Tristan wasn't holding on to going back for a punch. Tristan was aware of quite a number of running footsteps, toward them and away from them both, and things happened very fast after that.

8

POPPY

Poppy was happy to leave the actual fighting to people who knew what they were doing with it. She had a pretty good pointy elbow for breaking an unwanted grip, but when it came to throwing punches she knew she was out of her league.

Also, Tristan looked *really good*. For a second it seemed like Tristan would just make Daniel back down again, but then Daniel threw a punch and things got chaotic. People were screaming, other people were running—Poppy looked around for Daniel's guys and saw two of them rushing in, along with Peter, Tristan's fellow secret-agent, and airport security, plus a blond man in a suit followed by two guys in what looked like police or military uniforms...

Poppy's first instinct was to slip away, blend into the crowd and avoid getting mixed up in this. But she had started it—and it wasn't over yet, because she *still* didn't know what was in that bag.

Daniel had dropped the bag when he tried to punch Tristan. The fight was turning into a brawl—the guy in the gray jacket tried to jump Tristan from behind, but Peter was suddenly right there, getting in his way and getting punched before he could get a firm grip on the guy.

No one was watching Poppy. No one else seemed to have noticed the pink bag. It got kicked a little further away from the men fighting as more uniformed men rushed in, and Poppy circled around and picked it up, backing away to the shelter of a pillar before she pulled out the bouquet and tissue paper that filled the top of it.

There was silky underwear below that, a bunch of it, looking cheap and in colors that might have looked good on Sasha but wouldn't do Poppy any favors. Probably all Sasha's size, too, Poppy thought, absurdly annoyed. She pushed the lingerie to one side, trying to see what was below that.

Her hand brushed something solid, wrapped up in cloth and paper, and her breath caught.

Not a bomb, and not drugs, and not stolen jewelry. She knew that, even if she didn't know how she knew. What was in the bag was worth more than money; she could... she could *feel* something there, something almost magnetic, in the way it seemed to draw her hand to it.

It needed her.

Poppy didn't think. As if she'd practiced it a hundred times she flipped her raincoat over the bag to hide it, pulling up the wrapped-up objects—there were two or three, bundled carefully together. She shrugged her bag off her shoulder and moved the wrapped-up objects into it under the cover of her coat. She folded the raincoat on top, between the straps of the bag, and then stood and returned the bag to her shoulder, wrapping her arms around her waist and peeking out from behind the pillar toward the fight.

It was pretty well over now—Daniel and his two guys were face down with their wrists bound in plastic zip ties, and Tristan and Peter and the blond man in the suit were talking to the airport security people.

Tristan turned and met her eyes, as if he'd known

exactly where she was the whole time. He looked perfectly calm, his hair maybe a little more unruly than it had been, as if nothing had happened. Peter, beside him, was flushed pink and gesturing wildly.

"Poppy," Tristan said softly. "Come here, they need to see the pictures on your phone."

Only two of Daniel's guys had shown up. They had to find the third one. Poppy nodded and hurried over, aware of the weight of her bag on her shoulder all the time, aware of the stolen things that needed her, needed to be protected.

She pulled up the pictures and handed over her phone to Tristan. He put one arm protectively around her, so that her shoulder bag was tucked between them. That was all right, then. Tristan would help her keep them safe. She leaned into his shoulder, feeling the aftershock start to arrive. Tristan was talking in a language she didn't understand, and then—

"Poppy? Poppy, look at me—she needs to sit down somewhere quiet."

"The embassy car," someone said—the blond one in the suit, Poppy realized. He had a little pin on his lapel, the flag of Denmark. "It's just outside—we can sort out the rest of this without the young lady."

Tristan turned, guiding her back out of the terminal building. Poppy was vaguely aware that an assortment of people in uniforms were flanking them—she hoped Tristan wasn't in trouble—but then there was a long black car and Tristan was guiding her inside, following her in. The door closed, and they were alone.

"Well," Tristan murmured, brushing her hair back behind her ear. "That was quite a start to the day, wasn't it?"

Poppy nodded. She ought to tell him why she'd done it, ought to tell him about the things in her bag—she had to protect them—but right now she was shaking, and Tristan was protecting her, and the things along with her. So

85

maybe that was enough for right now.

"That's it," Tristan murmured, cuddling her close. Poppy breathed in the scent of him and tried not to be aware of anything else. "Catch your breath. You're safe now."

~~*

Eventually, when Poppy had pulled herself together a little, she and Tristan went back into the airport, this time to a security office. With Tristan on one side and the Danish embassy official—Poppy hadn't caught his exact title—on the other, everyone was polite to her, listening intently while she explained about Daniel being a bad news ex of Sasha's, and Poppy interfering because she was worried that he had some ulterior motive for luring Sasha away to Paris.

"Istanbul, as it turns out," one of the airport security guys said, shaking his head. "He had two one way tickets. You were right not to go anywhere with him, miss. We saw from the texts on your phone that he was still trying to get the other young lady involved as well, so we'll be checking up to make sure she's safe and see if she knows anything further that can help our investigation."

"Oh," Poppy said. She opened her mouth to say that she didn't think it had really been about what they seemed to think, but then she would have to explain about the... the things in her bag. They would take them from her, and they wouldn't understand. Poppy didn't even understand, really. She just *knew*.

She was distantly aware that this was crazy, but the instinct not to volunteer anything to the police, to get herself away, was stronger. They asked her a few more questions about Daniel and Sasha, promised to return her phone as soon as they could, and asked her to stay in London for the next few days so that they could contact her if they needed to ask follow up questions.

And that was it. It was really over; she went back out to the big embassy car with Tristan and the man from the embassy, and they drove away from the airport. Poppy leaned into Tristan's side and tried to ignore the feeling that nothing was over at all, that it was only just starting.

~~*

It was somehow surreal to arrive back at Tristan's posh hotel again after all that. She'd never really seen it in daylight. It was only midmorning now, though Poppy felt like an entire day ought to have gone by in the airport.

The hotel room was pristine again when they entered, Tristan's suitcase now neatly positioned on a luggage stand by one wall, Poppy's discarded dress from the night before hanging in the closet. Poppy didn't even want to guess what they'd done with her underwear—probably hand-washed it and put it away in a drawer with a scented sachet.

She peeked into the bathroom and saw that her hiking pack was now likewise resting on a luggage rack, while all the stuff she'd dumped out had been laid in tidy formation on the bathroom counter. Her bunny's head poked out of her fleece, which had been rewrapped around it so that it looked like a swaddled baby.

Everything seemed to be where it was supposed to be, but Poppy still had to do something about whatever she had stolen from Daniel, whatever it was that she was supposed to protect when she didn't even know what it was.

"Poppy?"

She turned to see Tristan standing near the connecting door to Peter's room. She didn't think Peter had come back from the airport with them, though she honestly wasn't sure she would have noticed unless he was sitting in Tristan's lap.

"I have to make a phone call," Tristan explained.

"Work, you know. They'll know I called out the embassy liaison, and they'll want to know why."

"Oh." Poppy felt her face heat. "I'm so sorry, Tristan, I didn't mean for you to—"

Tristan shook his head. "You're safe, that's all that matters. I promise, I didn't do anything I'll be in trouble for. But I have to report in. I hate to leave you, but..."

Poppy shook her head and gestured behind her. "I think I'm going to try out this gigantic bath. Maybe you could join me once you're done making secret agent phone calls?"

Tristan gave her one of his tiny smiles and nodded. "As soon as I can."

He stepped through into the adjoining room, closing the door firmly behind him, and Poppy stepped into the bathroom and shut the door, dropping to her knees and setting her shoulder bag down, yanking out everything else to unearth the wrapped-up objects at the bottom.

It was a single package, wrapped in a blue silk scarf. She pulled it into her lap, gently tugging the folds of cloth free.

The scarves fell away to reveal three paper-wrapped shapes. Poppy frowned down at them in her lap. Even though she couldn't see them yet, they seemed mismatched somehow. She touched each one in turn with the palm of her hand, and realized that two of them had the magnetism she had sensed, drawing her touch to them, while the other was inert, lifeless.

She unwrapped that one first, and stared in bemusement at a statuette of a bear, a little bigger than her two fists together. It was made of some unpolished crystal, almost colorless. It had the cool density of stone or glass, and it was competently made—she could see the bear's claws and teeth, and little marks to indicate the way the fur lay. She could see that it was hand-made, nothing that came from some souvenir factory, but there was no guessing how old it was. Given how Daniel had acted and all the cloak-and-dagger, she had to assume it was terribly old, and therefore terribly valuable.

Still, she couldn't help knowing that it was the least important of the three. She wrapped it back up in paper, settled it in her lap, and carefully unwrapped the next object.

Her breath caught as she stared down at the tiger in her hands.

Technically it was a carving of a tiger, much like the carving of the bear. This one was shaped from a pale amber-colored crystal, slightly clouded.

It didn't feel like the bear at all, though. It felt like the statuette was just a mask over the reality of an actual tiger. The weight of the massive beast, the heat and power of it, all was somehow balanced in her palms on a bed of crumpled paper.

She wanted to touch it, to stroke her finger down the smooth line of the back, shallowly incised with a tiger's stripes. She somehow knew that she would feel fur, and the motion of the tiger's breathing. But she felt too that it would be... rude, or something worse than that. Sacrilegious, to pet a tiger—especially *this* tiger—as if it were a housecat. This was no one's pet, nothing tame. This was a tiger.

No. *The* tiger.

And it was watching her. She felt its attention, heard a low growl that almost took the shape of words.

With shaking hands, Poppy wrapped the tiger back up in paper, thinking frantic apologies to it for caging it so. She lay it in her lap beside the carving of a bear that had no real bear inside it. She didn't even dare to unwrap the third statuette. She could feel the weight of it without that, and she didn't think she could withstand the presence of a... a lion, or whatever the next thing might be.

She looked around the bathroom, a little surprised somehow to find herself still in the same place she had been a few minutes before—or however long it had been, while she held the tiger in her hands.

Tristan would come looking for her soon. She still had no idea what the statues were, but at least now she knew what she had to research—where had the statues come from, when were they made and by whom? If she could figure that out, she could take them home where they belonged.

She wrapped them up again in the blue scarf and slipped them into her pack, hiding them with her clothes. She put the rest of her important stuff back into the pack while she was at it, letting that thought rattle around in her head.

She needed to take them home where they belonged. She still didn't know how she knew that, why she felt it so strongly—she didn't know what the tiger had been trying to say to her—but at least it was a goal, something she could figure out how to *do*.

They came from somewhere. They were old, and important—magical? Mystical? Had they been worshiped, somewhere? Why was the false bear with the real tiger and lion? Had they been looted by archaeologists or treasure hunters from their native home? If she could find out where they came from, she could take them back to where they were supposed to be.

For now, though, she closed up her pack and slipped out of her clothes. For now she was going to run a bath and wait for Tristan to come and find her.

The tiger and lion and bear were safe for now, and she would take them home as soon as she could. As soon as she had any idea where that might be.

Home. She shook her head and sat down on the edge of the huge tub. *I've never belonged anywhere. What do I know about going home?*

She would just have to figure it out.

9

TRISTAN

Tristan took a moment, after he shut himself in Peter's empty hotel room, to drag his thoughts away from Poppy to what he had to do next.

What he had told Poppy was not untrue—the involvement of the embassy staff would be reported to the Captain of the Guard sooner rather than later. Tristan had briefly reported in the night before, telling Magnus that Poppy had been located and was safe for the time being, so the news that some incident had occurred involving Tristan and Poppy wouldn't come as a total shock to Magnus.

But Tristan owed a report to Signy, who had sent him in search of her sister, and Kai, his oldest friend. He had a lot more to tell them than just a mission update.

He didn't know how to say it and make it sound the way it should, the way it felt, but there was no more time to put it off.

He tapped Kai's name and listened to the phone ring— only twice, and then Kai said, "Tristan? What's happened?"

Tristan closed his eyes, the corners of his mouth twitching up just a little. "Nothing. Nothing bad, anyway. But I need to tell you what's been happening—you and Signy, if she's near."

"Of course," Kai said, and Tristan heard the soft sounds of two people sitting down close to each other—snuggling, almost. He felt his distance from Poppy acutely and forced himself to focus.

"Tristan?" That was Signy. "Is everything all right?"

"That depends on your definition," Tristan replied slowly. "And whether it includes the prospect of having me as a brother-in-law."

He winced as soon as the words were out of his mouth—too level, too calm, conveying none of the delight and desire that filled him, down under his stony surface where he couldn't seem to let it out.

"We're delighted, of course," Kai said after a little pause, his voice almost as level as Tristan's. Kai had often done that, met him on his own ground in these things; it was how they had gotten to be friends to begin with.

Still, Tristan wished he could have said it right, and heard Kai say he was glad like he meant it.

After another second Signy burst out, like she'd been physically holding it back, "Tristan! Oh, I'm so glad!"

Tristan smiled a little then. "Thank you. But... Poppy doesn't sense it, you see. And on top of everything else... I don't want to rush her into any of it. If it were only the mission—"

"No, of course," Kai said quickly. "You have to take things in their own time. And there's still more than a week until the wedding."

Tristan nodded. It seemed like no time at all, but he hadn't even known Poppy an entire day yet. Surely in a week he could find the right way to tell her everything.

"And I don't want to rush her into going anywhere with me, especially," Tristan went on. "Because there was... a rather unpleasant scene this morning."

Tristan explained the business with Daniel in as few words as he could manage, emphasizing through it all that Poppy had never been in danger. Even without Tristan's intervention, she would have found a way to extricate herself.

"Still," Signy said. "I know she's probably been in situations like that so many times in the last year and we never knew a thing about it—but I'm so glad you were with her this time."

Tristan swallowed hard. "Me too. And I mean to always be, from now on."

There was a little pause—Tristan thought he could almost hear the silent communication between the pair on the other end—and then Kai said in a heavier tone, "Speaking as your Crown Prince, guardsman. You do recall your oaths. You require the king's permission to lay down your service to the Royal Guard, and until you do, you cannot take a mate, or have any family."

That rule had caused its share of grief for Kai and Signy before they had managed to obtain the king's permission around the interference of Otto and his schemes.

Somehow Tristan didn't think he and Poppy would face the same difficulties.

"Well," Tristan said slowly. "I still haven't completed my mission. Until Miss Zlotsky is returned to Valtyra, Your Highness, I am still required to proceed with my duties as a Royal Guard."

"Very true," Kai agreed, and then snorted, and Tristan could just picture his practiced straight face melting into a wide, bright grin. "I'll speak to the king about that, if you'll allow me to be your proxy? See if he can't arrange something effective upon your arrival in Valtyra with Poppy?"

Tristan couldn't help smiling, then, wide and obvious; it felt like being naked, and he was glad and sorry all at once that Kai couldn't see it. "Thank you, Kai."

"The least I owe you," Kai said firmly.

"Just one other thing, Tristan," Signy said. "Does Poppy... do you know if she even *has* her phone?"

Tristan closed his eyes again, thinking of what Poppy had told him the night before, thinking he knew nothing about her sister, about her sisterly jealousy all mixed up in love.

"She does have her phone," Tristan said slowly. "I believe she... wanted some time to think about her plans. I hope to influence those, of course, but..."

Tristan couldn't bring himself to say, *She's not in touch with you because she doesn't want to be,* but he knew Signy heard it, or something like it.

"Ah," she said quietly, and then more brightly, "Well, I look forward to hearing from her when she has some exciting news about the wonderful guy she met."

Tristan pictured the ways that could go and said, "Please... please tell me if she does, if it seems like she doesn't know yet that you already know?"

Signy blew out a breath. "Oh dear. Yes, of course. Maybe..."

"Don't second guess the man in the middle of things," Kai said gently. "He'll tell her when he can, and he won't lie to his own mate if push comes to shove."

Signy sighed. "Of course. Thank you for the news, Tristan, and I'm so happy for you both! I just... wish you were home, both of you."

"As soon as we can," Tristan promised.

When he had finished the call, he let himself wonder for a moment what home he and Poppy would really have in Valtyra. The Royal Guard had been all the home and family he'd had for all of his adult life; he had no intention of going back to the family he had renounced when he joined the Guard. They would never accept his human mate, and they would never forgive Tristan for leaving.

Would they live in the palace, by virtue of their closeness with the Crown Prince and Crown Princess? He was sure there would be plenty of work they could do, supporting Kai and Signy, but he doubted Poppy could be content for long in such a situation.

He thought longingly of that mountain lake from his dream, the curly-haired child holding Poppy's hand. Was there such a place for them somewhere, something that would be theirs in their own right?

Then he shook off those thoughts. It didn't matter where they ended up, or if they never ended up anywhere and wandered forever. His home was with Poppy, and every moment he spent worrying about the future instead of trying out that bath with her was a moment wasted.

~~*

The bath turned out to be excellent, as was the bed when they tried it again.

By late afternoon it was impossible to avoid being aware that he was *on vacation* with Poppy. His mission, such as it was, consisted only of wooing his mate and returning with her to Valtyra sometime in the next week or so. Once that was completed, he would no longer be a Royal Guard at all, and all his days would be his to fill as he chose.

"What you really need," Poppy informed him, looking him up and down when he had dressed so that they could go in search of a meal together. "Is *casual clothes*. I mean, I love the suits, but I cannot keep up with that style, and we're going to look like you're my bodyguard or something if we walk around with you dressed like that and me all backpack chic."

Shopping with Poppy turned out to be not unlike being outfitted by palace staff. Poppy was happy to select things for him and order him to try them on. Her method of checking fit was rather more... hands-on and thorough than any of the ladies at the palace had ever been, though.

None of them had ever looked at him the way Poppy did when he was finally wearing sufficiently tight jeans and a shirt that set off his coloring in a way she liked, either.

They were required to retire back to the hotel with their purchases, and wound up ordering in room service for supper.

Eventually.

~~*

Later that evening, after Tristan had left Poppy alone for five whole minutes to visit the bathroom, he came back to find her curled up in bed and frowning intently at her phone. It wasn't the one she'd surrendered at the airport—this one was in a hard black case that looked as if it could protect the device from just about anything.

Poppy was frowning intently into it, tapping and swiping at her screen with quick movements. Not the staccato of typing, as if she were messaging someone; she seemed to be looking for something.

"Poppy?"

She looked up at him and for just a second he could have sworn he saw a flash of guilt on her face before she smiled. "Sorry, just—I mean, I would love to hang out in bed forever, but... you have work to do, don't you? I was just looking up stuff to do so I could get out of your hair tomorrow. I was thinking about hitting some museums."

"Oh." Tristan came over to the bed, wondering how much he could confess—he couldn't just blurt out everything now, at the end of the day that had begun with Daniel trying to lure her off to Istanbul. But he had to tell her something, and he couldn't, must not, lie.

"Well, if you want some time to yourself, of course," Tristan said. "But I'm actually at a bit of a loose end. The mission I'm on is actually mostly resolved already, things happened much more quickly than anyone expected. Peter has taken on a lot of what's left." This was true; Peter had been liaising with the local law enforcement to make sure that Daniel was put away, and that Poppy wouldn't be troubled further.

"I've been granted some time to stay in London," Tristan went on, sitting down on the bed by Poppy, watching for her reaction. "I'm responsible for supervising Peter, to some extent, but I don't want to hover over him. So... I could accompany you, if you wished? I've never really traveled when I wasn't working. It might be nice to be a tourist. And I have the clothes for it now."

Poppy grinned. "Well, we can't let those jeans go to waste, that's for sure."

But a little frown crossed her face as she looked down at her phone again, though it vanished as soon as she returned her attention to him.

Tristan didn't press her on it, but he resolved not to push too much, if she expressed another wish to spend time alone. She didn't know she was his mate; she wouldn't feel the same pull he felt, the urge to be near her every moment. He had to let her have her space, or he would scare her away every bit as much if he simply blurted out the truth.

He didn't get much closer to figuring out how to tell her in the days that followed. They walked miles through Hyde Park and around the streets of London. Poppy told Tristan stories of her travels, both recently and as a child with her family. Tristan told her a little, too, about growing up in an isolated mountain village, about moving to the city as a young man, and some of the training he had gone through when he joined the Royal Guard.

He had to tell her, and soon. She was his mate, and he loved her, and he wanted her to understand what that meant. But when they were together he felt as if they already understood each other so well—Poppy never looked puzzled or hurt by his lack of expression, his inability to find the words for how he felt. She didn't try to match him, either; she just laughed and kissed him and it was if she already knew him, already saw all the things he was hiding.

She made it easy to forget that he had secrets, and he

forgot that there were things he didn't know about her, too.

He woke up one night to her tossing and turning in the throes of a nightmare, whispering frantically, "I will, I'm trying, I promise! I just don't know where it is, just tell me where to go—"

He had already drawn her into his arms, was already murmuring soothing words to her, when he realized that she had been speaking Valtyran.

10

POPPY

Poppy woke up to Tristan holding her close and asking urgently, "Can you hear me? Poppy?"

She nodded, reaching up to touch his face, the dream already fading. "Yes, yes."

Tristan's grip loosened, a strange expression—a strangely *obvious* expression—crossing his face, and she wondered if she had answered wrong somehow. Had he asked if she could hear him, or was it *can you understand me?* Or...

"Poppy," he said quietly, and then something slow and soft in what must be his native language. She could tell it was a question—the same question he had just asked?

"Sorry," she said, shaking her head. "Don't know that one."

He stared at her for a moment longer, brushing her hair back, and then he said, "Poppy, what were you dreaming about? You sounded frantic."

Poppy closed her eyes and cuddled closer to him, hiding her face.

The dreams of the tiger were getting intense and scary; she hadn't even unwrapped the statue to peek at it all day today, after last night's dreams, but tonight's had been worse, or at least... more.

The tiger never *did* anything to her in the dreams. It was just *there*, and it *needed her*, and she knew she had to do something, she had to get the tiger home, but she didn't know where that was. She hadn't been able to find anything online, or in any of the museums she'd visited, that looked anything like the carvings hidden in her pack.

She could almost hear the tiger growling, even now. It was getting impatient with her—or she was going *completely crazy*. And now Tristan was asking her a direct question, and God knew what she had said in her sleep.

She didn't want to lie to him. She should have told him days ago about the statues. She kept waiting for someone to show up and ask her about them, but it seemed that somehow no one had noticed what she did at the airport.

How could she tell Tristan she'd stolen the contraband Daniel had tried to make her smuggle for him? How could she tell him the contraband was an ancient mystical tiger carving and its friends, and they *needed her*?

Unfortunately, that made it difficult to think of what to say to Tristan now. She was still so shaken from the dream, tired and worried and she could *still hear the tiger growling*.

"It's just... something I have to do." Poppy whispered finally. "In the dream, there's... there's something I have to do, but I don't know how to do it."

"Who tells you that you have to do it, in the dream?" Tristan asked quietly. "It seemed like you were trying to explain to someone, or arguing with them."

"It was just a dream," Poppy said, but she almost choked on the lie, and she could have sworn the tiger growled louder. She could almost hear words in it. *Do not deny us. Take us home.*

"Poppy, if there's something you have to do," Tristan

said softly. "I only want to help. If you tell me about it, maybe I can help."

Poppy breathed in through her nose, out through her mouth. She couldn't think of any words to say that weren't a lie, that wouldn't make the tiger angry. *More* angry.

There was only one thing that she could say that was true, one thing she'd been holding back and needed Tristan to know right now.

"I love you," she whispered, and it came out strangled, like she was scared, when it was the one thing about all this that she was sure of. The one thing she relied on.

She had known from the moment they met that she felt something about him that she hadn't ever felt about anyone else. The last few days had only made it clearer.

Traveling with someone, being in a strange place with them, showed you a lot about who they really were. She didn't need to know Tristan's last name; she'd already watched him cope with being made to try on clothes and inexplicable Tube station closures and Poppy's unexplained obsession with the archaeology section of every museum in London over the last few days.

She knew him. She knew what they had. She loved Tristan so much, and she couldn't bear to lose him to what she'd done, or whatever was wrong with her.

Tristan pushed her back enough that he could look into her eyes, and she forced herself to meet his gaze. He studied her for a long, still moment in the early light, and then he said, "I love you, Poppy. And I won't stop loving you, or wanting to protect you."

Poppy put her hands over her face, feeling an echo of the shakiness she had felt that night outside the club, and at the airport after Daniel was arrested the adrenaline hitting her after the danger was over. She hadn't known Tristan long, but she knew that he meant what he said. He knew that he was serious about her, serious about this. When Tristan said *I won't stop loving you*, that was a promise she could trust.

And she had to trust someone, because she was getting absolutely nowhere on her own.

"I did something," she whispered. "That day at the airport, I... I did something and I didn't tell the police. And I didn't tell you. And I—I don't want to get you into trouble with the embassy and everyone, but I don't know what to do."

"Tell me, Poppy." Tristan pulled her closer again. "I'll listen. I'll help if I can. We can solve this."

"I..." Poppy could think of words. "I took something. Daniel was trying to smuggle them, I think, that's why he wanted me or Sasha to go with him. The pink bag, you remember?"

Tristan squeezed her tight and nodded against her hair.

Poppy opened her mouth to try to describe what was inside, but no words came, or... strange words wanted to come, pushing her mouth into shapes she didn't recognize.

"It's easier if I show you," Poppy said finally, pushing against Tristan's grip. Tristan let her go, only keeping hold of her hand, and let her lead him out of bed. He turned on the bedside lamp and followed her to her hiking pack, brought out of the bathroom now and set tidily on a luggage stand beside his suitcase.

Poppy knelt, and Tristan knelt beside her. Poppy was dimly aware that they were naked, and wondered if they shouldn't be—but then, the tiger was naked too, wasn't he?

"Okay," Poppy said, half to herself and reached into the pack. She didn't have to look to know when she touched the scarf-wrapped shape of the tiger; she could feel it.

Tristan would understand, anyway, once she showed him. He would know they were important, just like she had known. It had to be obvious, didn't it? Daniel had known they were valuable.

Poppy's hands moved quickly, almost outside her conscious control, as she pulled out and unwrapped the tiger. Now that she was so close, she couldn't wait to see it again, to feel the presence of the tiger, to maybe really understand it instead of just hearing that growl echoing around in her head. As she had before, she peeled the paper back, not touching it with her bare hands.

The tiger seemed to glow with its own light, the amber holding some memory of sunlight. Poppy felt more strongly than ever the urge to touch, and the urge to bow down before this powerful presence.

Tristan made a strange, choked-off noise, and Poppy frowned at the realization that he was gripping both of her hands, holding them away from touching the tiger. She raised her head to look at him, and he was looking at the statue instead.

"See?" Poppy said. "Do you understand, now?"

"No, I don't," Tristan said.

He met Poppy's eyes and she could see he didn't. He was confused, worried, but it wasn't hard for him to look away from the tiger, to resist touching it.

"Let go," she said, though that wasn't what she meant to say. And it wasn't the way she meant to say it, the words turned oddly in her mouth.

Tristan frowned harder and shook his head. He made a quick move, so that he was holding both her wrists in one hand; she started to scream when his other hand went toward the tiger—he couldn't, he mustn't touch it, he wasn't—wasn't—

She cut off as he flipped the wrappings back over it and pushed it off her lap. It was like the air clearing, suddenly, the way the frantic panic evaporated. She could breathe. She could *think*.

"Oh, shit," Poppy said, looking at the tiger, and then toward her pack, where the lion and the false bear waited.

"Poppy, what was that?"

"It's a tiger," Poppy said, forcing herself to meet his eyes, hoping that he would, somehow, believe her. "I know it's just a carving, but when I look at it... it's really a tiger. I can feel it."

"A tiger who speaks Valtyran," Tristan said, sounding... much less surprised than he should, and...

"What?" Poppy looked over at him. "Valtyran? What..."

"That's the language you were speaking," Tristan said. "When you asked me if I understood. When you told me to let go. And when you dreamed of the tiger and told it you didn't know where to go."

"You knew..." Poppy looked from Tristan to the wrapped bundle, remembered Tristan asking her that question as soon as she woke up. For a second, when he asked, she had still understood, but then it was gone. When the tiger left her.

"I don't understand," Poppy said slowly. "Do you know what the tiger is?"

"I think so," Tristan said. "But I'm not sure what it's doing to you."

Poppy blinked. "Oh, God, it's not evil, is it? Like a Ring of Power?"

Tristan frowned seriously. "I don't know anything about that, have you encountered one before?"

Poppy stared at him. "Yes," she said finally. "In movies. *The Lord of the Rings?* One Ring to rule them all?"

Tristan's face went very blank. "Ah. No. I don't think the tiger is evil. But I do think it's powerful, and perhaps... less well-behaved than it ought to be. And I think you're drawn to it. Aren't you?"

Poppy nodded slowly.

"You want to protect it?" Tristan prompted. "To keep it for yourself, or...?"

Poppy shook her head quickly. "I need to take it home. It needs to go home. To the people it belongs to."

Tristan nodded, his expression easing very slightly, and he turned toward her. "Come here. Let me help. I think if you're touching me when you look at it, it won't affect you so strongly."

Poppy crawled into Tristan's lap, relaxing into the warmth and comfort of his touch, even though she had no idea how it might help, and she still didn't understand how Tristan could look at it and know.

He didn't think she was crazy, though, and he wasn't angry about her stealing the tiger. So they were off to a pretty good start.

He wrapped his arms around her, set his chin on her shoulder, and said, "Okay. Now try again."

Poppy reached out with a shaking hand and tugged the silk free of the tiger. She gasped at the feeling of the tiger's presence—it was different this time, as if she were watching the tiger from a little distance. Safely held in Tristan's arms, she knew that she could touch the stone if she needed to, but she could also just lean closer to peer at it, getting comfortable with the feeling of the tiger's presence.

It didn't growl at her this time, but she thought she could almost hear it breathing.

"Now do you feel it?" Poppy asked. "The tiger?"

Tristan shook his head. "It's strange. I can tell that there's something—pulling on you, almost. But it just looks like a carving to me. Is this why you've been going to so many museums? Trying to find something like it?"

Poppy nodded. "But there's nothing. And I've never even heard of... what did you say the language is called? Valtyran? Where does that come from? And how can I—" Poppy stumbled over the words. "What, am I speaking Valtyran now?"

Tristan's grip on her tightened. "You are. The tiger is trying to help you, but he's probably not quite sure what to make of you."

Poppy nodded. She could feel that now that she wasn't so overwhelmed by the tiger's existence. It was *puzzled* by her. "I have to take them home."

"Yes. You're their guardian," Tristan murmured. "You're a Guardian of the Stones."

Poppy twisted in his grip. She could hear the capital letters. *In Valtyran*, because they were both speaking Valtyran now. "Tristan, what does that mean? What are they? What—"

What am I? What are you?

Tristan was still looking at the tiger. He had an odd, hungry expression, a more open expression than she'd seen from him outside of bed; she might have been tempted to feel jealous, but when he looked at her his expression was just as open. His eyes were wondering, his lips slightly parted, as if *she* were something magical.

"They come from my country. Valtyra. They were stolen long ago, before I was born—the Wisdom Stones," and in English he added, "Stones, you know, like the stone of a cherry?" before he went on in Valtyran. "The center, the seed. And Wisdom, in the old language, cunning—it was another way of saying magic. The secret knowing of something."

Poppy stared at him. "So they're from... Denmark."

Tristan closed his eyes. "No. I travel on diplomatic papers from Denmark, due to certain longstanding treaties between my country and Denmark, but... no. I come from Valtyra, and so do the stones, and we should take them back there as soon as possible. We should get *you* there as soon as possible."

"Tristan..." Poppy twisted, pushing half away from him. She agreed with him, she needed to take the stones home, but why was Tristan suddenly able to tell her this stuff as soon as he knew she had them? "If you're not an agent from Denmark—you're from some, some secret, magic country—"

It wasn't much, just a tightening of his face, a darkness flashing through his amber eyes, but Poppy saw the guilty flinch that meant she was hitting close to home.

"What was your *mission*?" Poppy demanded. "You said it was sensitive, important, and then you said it was taken care of and you were just keeping an eye on Peter, except then you see these stones and all of a sudden it's time to go?"

"My mission wasn't anything to do with the stones," Tristan said. "My mission was to find you."

"Me," Poppy repeated. She covered up the tiger and tucked it back into her pack, then moved away from Tristan completely, folding her arms over her chest. "Me, the Guardian of the Stones?"

"*A* Guardian," Tristan corrected. "There are others. But—no. You, Poppy Zlotsky." He grimaced and added, "I did ask you why you said your sister sent me."

"My..."

Signy. Signy and her fabulous European guy. Signy and her carefully non-specific location. *Valtyra*, the secret country.

Poppy backed away from Tristan, grabbing a blanket from the bed and wrapping it around herself as she stood. She felt sick, exposed, and somehow she still wanted to go to Tristan, to have him hold her and make it okay.

But Tristan had lied to her. "So this was all just—"

"No," Tristan said quickly. "No, Poppy, I didn't pretend anything, I swear to you. I—when I saw you, I knew. The same way you knew what the tiger was as soon as you saw it, I knew *you*. I knew you were meant for me— we're meant for each other. I told you I was serious. I told you I didn't want to go too fast and scare you. But I knew the moment I looked into your eyes."

Poppy turned to look at him. She wasn't even angry, she just wanted him to be telling her the truth. She wanted to believe that the important parts of this were real, that even if he had kept things from her, she knew the parts of him that mattered. She knew *Tristan*, even if she didn't know all this stuff about Valtyra and Guardians and Stones.

"How? You—you can't tell about the stones. How could you tell about me?"

Tristan smiled a little. "I'm a little special too. I... I

could show you, if it will help you believe me." She could see him struggling with something. She could *see it*, right on his face, not in tiny motions but something naked, something he was letting her see. "Please, let me show you."

Poppy nodded sharply.

Tristan took a breath, closed his eyes, and... *changed*. Her eyes couldn't quite follow it, but a second later Tristan—the Tristan she knew—was gone, and in his place was a tiger. An actual living, breathing tiger, not just the unseen presence of one. He looked at her with the same amber eyes, his tail twitching a little and his ears tilting toward her.

Poppy moved toward him in a daze, reaching out slowly with both hands. She couldn't be scared—not after feeling the presence of the tiger in the stone. Tristan was just the same, but he was a tiger she really could see and touch. She ran a hand over the soft fur of his face, behind one ear, and the enormous tiger let out a rumble like a diesel engine.

Poppy jerked her hand back, laughing a little in surprise and delight. He was a tiger—or could become a tiger, at least, since he was obviously also human most of the time. Tristan was *magic*.

He sat back on his haunches and then changed again, becoming her familiar Tristan with his smooth brown skin and glossy black curls, his familiar scars. He grinned widely at her, showing all his blunt human teeth. "That's how I knew, Poppy. I'm that kind of special—most of us who are, we can sense our mates when we meet them."

Poppy ran a hand through her hair, trying to get her head around all of that. "You're a shapeshifting tiger, from a secret country you're a secret agent for. *And* you know my sister. And she sent you here to find me? And you didn't think you needed to *tell me any of that?* What made you think that was okay?!"

By the end she was maybe screaming a little.

Tristan swept an arm toward the pack where the stones were tucked away. He might have gotten his human shape back, but his calm façade hadn't come with it. "I don't know, maybe the same reason you didn't want to tell me you were carrying stolen property *with a tiger spirit inside it?*"

"That's not the same!"

Poppy knew, even as the words came out of her mouth, that at some point she was going to have to tell him about the lion. And the bear.

"It's *exactly the same!* You didn't want me to think you were crazy, or a thief, and I didn't want you to think I was—" Tristan waved his arms wildly. "Terrifying, or evil, since that seems to be all you've ever heard about magic before!"

"Oh my God don't bring *The Lord of the Rings* into this!" Poppy yelled back, stepping forward to shove him away from the pack and the stones, though pushing on him was like pushing on a wall of rock. "Changing into a *tiger* is a whole different ball game! How do I even know you—"

Tristan moved suddenly, catching her wrists and ducking to kiss her hard.

Poppy gasped, then moaned, feeling the same rush she always got from touching him. It felt like more somehow, now, knowing the tiger was there within him, restrained behind his human form. Knowing that what was between them was true magic, and not just something she was rushing into that might turn out to be a mistake later on.

Knowing that he was her—what had he called it?—her *mate.*

"That," Tristan said against her lips, breathing hard, his hands still holding tight to her wrists. "That's how you know. You feel it, and you know what's true."

Poppy was breathless, her whole body tingling and hot. "Show me. Show me, make me feel—"

Tristan scooped her up and threw her down on the bed, following right after her. She reached for him, but he caught her wrists again, holding her down as he kissed her, rough and claiming.

"Mine," he whispered. "You're mine, Poppy, my mate, and that's all that matters here. You belong with me. Whatever else we are, whatever else is true, nothing is more true than this. We belong together."

"Show me," Poppy insisted, trying to wrap her legs around him, to hurry him along.

Tristan growled against her throat, biting and sucking at the tender skin there. Poppy could only tip her head back and let him, knowing how easily she would show his marks. She wanted them—wanted something tangible, some sign that she belonged to him. She gasped his name, begging for more, and Tristan settled lower over her, letting her feel his weight and still holding her down.

She could feel how hard he was, the length of him pressing hot against her belly. She felt her own pulse pounding between her legs where she was wet for him, needing him inside her. She tilted her hips up against him—this was no time for taking it slow.

Tristan groaned and moved to line them up. He teased for a moment, rubbing his hardness against her without pushing inside, and Poppy gasped and snarled at him, arching up against his hold. She couldn't break it, though. She couldn't run away from this, couldn't control it. She was his now.

Poppy cried out as Tristan pushed into her, fast enough for her to feel the ache of stretching around him. She was coming almost as soon as he was inside her, and he ducked his head to her breast, biting kisses all over her as she came in shuddering waves, clenching around his erection inside her.

He started to move only when she stopped, just rocking his hips at first and building up to thrusts. It was intense, right on the edge of too much, the pleasure edged with pain, but Poppy pushed up into every thrust, welcoming him and wanting more. Soon he was giving it to her, pounding her into the bed as he took her, letting her feel the wild strength of him.

Her pleasure built up again, a storm tide of feeling, as her mate moved in her and over her. His lips found hers again just as he found an angle that made her scream, and it wasn't long before she was tipping over the edge again.

This time he came with her, nothing between them. She felt him move a last few times inside her, and when he went rigid she could feel his hardness pulsing in her, the hot wetness as he spilled inside her.

Good, she thought, before she could think anything coherent about it. It felt right to have nothing between him, to have him inside her in the deepest, most intimate possible way. *My mate.*

For a while they were both still, catching their breath. Poppy was floating in a dazed kind of bliss that felt a lot like she'd just done something a little death-defying. She might have bruises later, but for now it just felt so *good*, like Tristan was a mountain she'd climbed or a choppy bay she'd swum across.

Except, now, wherever she went, whatever adventures she had, he would be at her side.

Poppy opened her eyes and found Tristan watching her. She went to touch his face and realized his hands were still clasped around her wrists.

He let go instantly, a sheepish look crossing his features. "Sorry. Forgot I was holding on."

Poppy ran her fingers down his uninjured cheek, and then, carefully watching for any sign that it was unwelcome, down the scars on the other.

"I don't mind you holding on," Poppy said quietly. "I don't want you letting me go."

Tristan shook his head and then kissed her, just a brush of lips. "Did I hurt you?"

Poppy shook her head, glancing down at herself. She could already see red marks rising on her breasts, and she knew there would be more on her throat.

With a smirk, she said, "It looks worse than it feels, I

promise. Pale skin shows everything, that's all."

Tristan moved lower, kissing gently down her throat and her breasts before he lay down beside her, tugging her over to face him with one arm and leg over her, as if she might run away. Poppy reached up and twined her fingers into his hair, just to let him know he wasn't going anywhere either.

"I'm sorry I didn't tell you sooner," Tristan said softly. "About being sent to find you, and your sister, and everything. I was told not to force you, but also to make sure you were there in time for the wedding. And not to lie to you but not to ruin all the surprises."

Poppy squinted at him. "Oh God, that sounds like my mom is there too."

Wait, he'd said *wedding*.

Well. She probably wouldn't mind seeing Signy getting married to her perfect guy now that she really had found her own.

"Both your parents, yes," Tristan said. "But I should have realized that I had to trust you more than I worried about what they said. You're my mate. I'll be leaving the king's service as soon as we're back in Valtyra, but you're the rest of my life."

Poppy bit her lip, trying to hold back a grin. She could feel a laugh bubbling up, though she knew Tristan was utterly serious. She nodded, not trusting herself to speak without sounding like she didn't believe him, or didn't feel the same. It was hard to imagine the rest of her life, the way Tristan said it. It was hard to imagine knowing where she would be, and who she would be with, in a year, let alone decades from now.

Tristan gave her one of his microscopic smiles and kissed her lightly. "I see I shall have to be serious enough for both of us."

"I'm *serious!*" Poppy insisted, bursting into helpless giggles in the middle of the word. She pecked little kisses all over Tristan's face as she said, "I mean it! I'm committed too!"

When Tristan actually grinned back, sudden and bright as the sun coming up, she knew he understood, and maybe even believed her. If he didn't, well. He planned on sticking around, so he'd have plenty of time to see that she wasn't running away from him.

She stopped giggling and snuggled closer. Tristan's arms closed tight around her.

"So I guess I don't need to convince you to go up to the Ashmolean today," she mumbled against Tristan's chest.

Tristan sighed. "No. And we really should get you, and the stones, home soon. You'll be safer there."

"Safe...?" Poppy frowned, and then the realization caught up with her all at once.

Daniel had had a very specific plan to travel to Istanbul with the stones. He had been delivering them, or selling them, to someone. Someone who, if they could get in touch with Daniel, would know she had the stones. They might not know exactly where she had gone, but...

"I'll protect you," Tristan promised softly. "That's what I'm here to do. We just need to get to the airport and get to Valtyra. You'll be safe there."

Poppy nodded against his chest, and Tristan added, "You should probably get dressed first."

Poppy nodded, but she let herself cling to him for another moment before she got out of bed to do it.

11

TRISTAN

Before Tristan had persuaded himself to get out of bed, let alone Poppy, there was a loud, rapid knock on the door from Peter's room. Peter's voice accompanied it, sharp and urgent, "Tristan?"

Tristan got up immediately, and Poppy was already scrambling away, grabbing her pack and slamming the bathroom door behind her. Heart beating fast, from startlement and Poppy's instantaneous reaction, Tristan called out, "What is it, Peter?" as he approached the door.

"I need to speak to you," Peter replied, his voice lower, but Tristan still had no trouble making out either his words or the tension behind them. "About... work."

Tristan unlocked the door and yanked it open, giving Peter a quick glance before turning away to find clothes. Peter was fully dressed in a suit, but he looked slightly disheveled, like he'd been wearing the suit for hours and all of them had been busy.

Tristan felt a twinge of guilt—he really should have been keeping a closer eye on Peter, he had no idea where Peter had been this morning—as well as a deeper unease.

115

Peter had inserted himself into the investigation into Daniel's actions. Tristan had assumed it was to have something to do, to prove himself by keeping busy and pursuing the man who had endangered Poppy.

Now that Tristan knew what Daniel had been smuggling, though, it was hard not to make a guess at who would want the wisdom stones. Otto had to be at the top of the list, and it was only a few weeks ago that Peter had attempted to kill Princess Signy, had left the marks of his claws on Tristan and Kai, because Otto had told him to.

For the smuggling to be happening so quickly, when Otto had fled Valtyra only days ago, in what had seemed to be utter disarray...

Otto had to have known already how he could get his hands on the stones. He might even have been behind the original theft, years ago. A man who thought so far ahead, who laid such intricate plans, wouldn't have had any trouble coaching Peter on what to say if captured to win the sympathy of the king and the rest of the Royal Guard. It was Peter who had brought them to London—not just in time to meet Poppy, but the night before the smuggling was supposed to be done.

Tristan was confident that nothing he was thinking showed in his face or body as he turned his back on Peter and walked across the room, but he still felt a little better when he had pants on. He turned back toward Peter as he pulled on an undershirt.

"What's going on? I told Poppy about Valtyra this morning—we're headed back there as soon as we can get a flight plan filed."

Peter's mouth tightened, and he folded his arms. Tristan planted his own feet at the sight of that unspoken resistance. He was between Peter and Poppy—between Peter and the stones. He would not be moved.

"I agree," Peter said, leaving Tristan feeling a little off balance, though he showed nothing. "Miss Zlotsky needs to be removed from the country and safe in Valtyra as soon as possible. Some... precautions in transit may be required, though, and... questions have arisen due to developments in the case."

Tristan stared at him. Peter was speaking English, whether out of habit from working with the English police for the last few days, or because he was just as aware as Tristan was that Poppy was directly behind the closed bathroom door, listening with all her might.

Still, it wasn't the sort of English Tristan had ever heard him speak before. Peter was speaking *Police*.

"Tell me what happened," Tristan directed firmly.

Peter blew out an irritated breath and for once *didn't* shoot a guilty look at Tristan's face. "Daniel was attacked early this morning, while being transferred from short-term lockup to a jail. By a bird."

Tristan blinked, but took Peter's meaning instantly. "By a shifter."

Peter nodded sharply. "Went straight for the face and throat. He'll live, but no one's sure he'll speak again." Peter's gaze did flick to Tristan's scars then, but it was an oddly neutral acknowledgment of their presence, nothing more. "I found out about this when a new detective showed up—a shifter, some kind of stag, I think. We spotted each other immediately, obviously, and I had to call out the embassy to keep from being suspected of being involved, but eventually he let me in on what happened, and we took a look at CCTV footage from the airport."

Tristan turned away, looking for a clean shirt. He knew how the rest of the revelation was going to go.

"He was smuggling something, Tristan. For shifters, who very nearly killed him for not delivering. And whatever it was he had, it looks like Miss Zlotsky took it. Diplomatic immunity will keep her out of jail, but it won't protect her from whoever sent that hawk after Daniel— and he was heard to scream *the girl took them* before he ceased to be able to form words, so they'll be looking for her."

Tristan buttoned up his shirt very neatly and picked up his tie. He could sense Poppy in the bathroom, keeping very still. He hoped she was letting him handle this, and not asking the tiger stone for help.

"Tristan," Peter said sharply. "Diplomatic immunity or no, Detective Sunderland is waiting downstairs to find out what the hell Miss Zlotsky took. You have to—"

"I have to keep her safe, and bring her back to Valtyra," Tristan said evenly. "You were seconded to *me* to support that mission. Remember?"

Peter's eyes narrowed. "So, what, I was supposed to sit here and twiddle my thumbs and wait for you to quit being too mate-blinded to step foot outside? That's what I'm here for?"

"I have no idea what you're here for, Peter." Tristan turned fully to face him as he shrugged into his jacket. "I only know that you've said some things."

Peter's hands closed into fists, his face flushing with rage, and Tristan watched him, waiting for some sign he could be sure of.

"You think I—I—why would I still be here?" Peter demanded. "Why would you even—if you thought that I was really a traitor, why even let me out of that cell? Why would I surround myself with *police*—"

"Who don't know the country you betrayed even exists," Tristan put in.

"*I was lied to,*" Peter snarled, crossing the room in quick strides that wanted to be a single, furious pounce. "You heard my confession, Tristan. You—you said you—"

And there it was, a flicker of hurt in the anger.

"You said you thought I could start again," Peter whispered, almost a hiss. In Valtyran, now. Nothing about this was habit, or intended for Poppy's ears. "I've been doing nothing but trying to solve this, to make sure Miss Zlotsky and—and anyone else like her are never endangered by that man again. I'm telling you the truth,

I'm telling you I'll help get her out of England. Why would you doubt me now?"

Tristan watched his eyes, hoping his own instincts couldn't really be as wildly mistaken as all that, and said, "Because I know what Poppy took. And I know who would want it."

Peter's expression turned to bafflement. "What, you think... Otto? What would he..."

Peter trailed off, and then his gaze sharpened all at once, going from Tristan to the door. "You mean—but—she's human, she'd never even heard of Valtyra, how—"

The bathroom door opened behind Tristan, and he edged a little further into Peter's space. It was pointless to try to tell Poppy to stay back.

"Since we're talking about me," Poppy said, in flawless Valtyran. "I thought I'd join in. Here, look, this is what I took, okay? I was curious and then realized they were important. I didn't have to know anything about Valtyra to figure that out."

Peter's jaw dropped. Tristan managed to restrain his own expression of surprise to looking to see which of the statues Poppy was holding. He didn't feel anything pulling at her, the way the tiger had when it was unwrapped under her hands, and she seemed much too calm.

He stopped breathing when he saw what Poppy was holding in her hands, offering it to Peter like it was nothing. It was another Wisdom Stone—the *bear*, the stone—the *heart*—of the king's own clan and the royal line.

Tristan forced his gaze to Peter. If Otto wanted any of the stones at all, he would want this one most. He would want to destroy it, or subvert it, use it to destroy the af Bjorn clan in Valtyra. There wasn't much left of them anyway—the royal family coming down to Princess Signy was only one example. And Signy's children would probably be lions, not bears, so that was another line extinguished.

What Poppy held in her hands could change all that, if

it was taken home safely—or hasten it, fatally, if Otto got his hands on it.

Tristan saw a flicker of greed in Peter's eyes. Dragons were always that way; they couldn't help thinking of their hoards and what they could add to them all the time. Serving in the Royal Guard, Peter was allowed to declare, if challenged, *I keep a king.* It was vital to say *keep*, not *own* or even *hold*, but the keeping of the king was considered, officially, to outrank any other hoard regardless of its content.

I keep the Wisdom Stone of the royal lineage—or better yet, *I own*—would be an unimaginable temptation to a disgraced dragon, without family or clan or hoard of any kind.

Peter squeezed his eyes shut, blowing out a breath like a hiss, hot enough that Tristan felt its passage. "You need to be Valtyran to understand that you shouldn't just wave it around in people's faces, apparently. Do you have any idea—"

Poppy's gaze darted to Tristan as soon as Peter's eyes closed, and she made a face—apologetic and sure, all at once—and Tristan thought that he knew exactly why Poppy was waving the stone around like it meant nothing. Even if she had some particular connection with the tiger, the bear wouldn't—couldn't mean nothing to her, and she wasn't that good at pretending. Not good enough to fool her mate, even if she might have fooled Peter.

The bear was fake. Empty. There was nothing inside to communicate with her.

"Clearly I have no idea," Poppy said breezily. "Just like I have no idea who this Otto guy is and how you betrayed Valtyra. But I'd like to know both of those things before I listen to another word either of you have to say."

Peter ran a hand through his hair, turning half away.

"Otto attempted to overthrow the king of Valtyra," Tristan said quietly. "Your sister was instrumental in stopping him. Otto was a Count, and First Minister on the King's Council. He had a lot of people fooled—including

Peter. And at his urging, Peter attempted to stop your sister."

Poppy frowned, and then her gaze dropped to Tristan's scars and darted to Peter. "When you say *stop*..."

"Kai didn't let him hurt her, and I didn't let him get away," Tristan said firmly, stepping smoothly between them when Poppy lunged, raising the bear stone as though it were nothing but a rock. She obviously intended to bring it down on Peter's skull, but Tristan got his arms around her and bore her a few steps back from Peter.

The stone really had to be false; she never would have used the real one that way.

Poppy's attention shifted from Peter to Tristan as soon as he thwarted her. "And you! Why didn't you tell me Signy was in danger?! Why didn't you tell me that *he* did *that* to you?"

Tristan raised his eyebrows enough for Poppy to know he was being pointed about it. "There hasn't been much time, my own. And I didn't think he was a danger to anyone. I still don't. I think he is doing his best to make things right."

Poppy pressed her lips together and then brandished the bear at him. "Fine. But you'd better give some serious thought to what secrets you're still keeping from me, Mister, because I'm not giving you many more free passes on that."

Tristan considered, for a split second, laying it all out right now—that Signy's father had been a prince of Valtyra, Signy a princess from birth, now the Crown Princess, and likely Queen before very much longer, with Kai ruling at her side.

There was no time, not if someone knew Poppy had the stones, if they were sending shifters to attack. He glanced toward the windows, the drapes still drawn over them, and then met Poppy's eyes again. "I understand. But we need to go. *Now*."

Poppy nodded, and Tristan turned to find Peter

watching him with an expression Tristan couldn't read. More positive than not, he thought, and that was progress. He moved to lay his hand on Peter's shoulder and squeezed. "Do you need more than that to tell your detective? Because I'd like to have his help as well as yours to get Poppy to the airport."

Peter blinked at him, smiled tentatively, and then said, "I think I can work with that."

12

POPPY

Poppy hesitated before returning the bear stone to her pack. She'd been willing to wave it at Peter because she was—mostly—sure that it was fake, but she couldn't be *entirely* sure.

Tristan said she was a guardian and that was why she could hear the tiger, but it wasn't like she'd had testing or training on it. She might not be a very *good* guardian, or it might take a different kind of skill to hear a bear rather than the big cats. Maybe the bear was hibernating.

Still, she could see that they were relying on Peter to get out of here and back to Valtyra safely with the tiger and lion, so she thought a show of trust was probably in order. She turned back at the door to the bathroom and held out the bear stone again.

"Do you need this one?" Poppy asked. "To show the police, or... whatever?"

Peter stared at the stone, and Tristan went very, very still. Poppy had a feeling she'd stuck her foot in it in some way she didn't really understand, but she held her position, waiting for some cue from Tristan.

Finally Peter shook his head. "No. No, it... it belongs to Valtyra, and for the time being I..." Peter looked toward Tristan. "I don't think I'm coming home anytime soon."

Poppy turned her back and hurried to put the bear away safely with the others, still listening to the men outside.

Tristan spoke first. "Peter, if this is going to make trouble for you with the police here—"

Peter laughed a little, with a bitter edge. "No, it's not that. If Otto was behind this somehow—I have to stay, don't you see? I have to help with the investigation. I *can* help better than anyone else in Valtyra. And we both know I'd have been called home days ago if anyone in Valtyra had the slightest use for me. It's better this way, Tristan. I can prove myself before I come home."

Poppy finished rearranging everything in her pack to make it fit with the stones inside and closed it up, slinging it on her shoulder. But she hesitated until she heard Tristan sigh and say, "Well, I'm not going to tell you not to. Magnus approved you helping with the investigation for as long as we were in town, didn't he?"

"Yes," Peter said firmly. "So as long as I stay, I'm still seconded."

Poppy stepped into the doorway before Tristan could feel compelled to try to say anything supportive. "I'm ready."

Tristan gave her a tiny smile, like he knew that she had timed her entrance for him, and picked up his own suitcase. "Let's go, then."

Peter led them to a freight elevator, and when the doors opened there were already several people inside— four in police uniforms, two men and two women, and a man in a suit who introduced himself as Detective Inspector Sunderland.

"These constables are on our in-the-know team," Sunderland said, gesturing to the uniformed police. "So they won't be shocked by anything they see. We'll escort you directly to the airport." Sunderland looked Poppy up and down and then looked at Peter. "As for the matter of the items in question...?"

"Sacred artifacts, now being repatriated," Peter said briskly. "I'll write up a full report, but suffice to say that Miss Zlotsky was acting on behalf of my country and shall have the full backing and protection of the Kingdom."

Sunderland gave Peter a look like he was going to expect a *lot* of explanation for that, later, but in the meantime the elevator doors opened into a parking garage, where the Embassy car and three police cars awaited them. Tristan guided Poppy quickly into the Embassy car and Peter and Sunderland joined them while the police dispersed to the other cars.

Poppy put on her seatbelt and then wrapped her arms very firmly around her pack. Tristan put one arm over her shoulders, and murmured in her ear, "We're not going to let any harm come to you."

Poppy looked toward him, her eyes going to his scars. "Like you didn't let anything happen to Signy?"

"No," Tristan said, tightening his grip. "Because that was my duty, and you are far more than that."

Poppy closed her eyes and leaned into Tristan's grip for the rest of the ride to the airport.

She opened her eyes when Tristan's grip on her tightened further, and she realized that they were driving into a different part of the airport than she'd ever seen before.

"We're not walking through the terminal," Tristan explained quietly. "They're driving us direct to the plane on the tarmac. That means we'll be in the open for a minute, going from the car up into the plane, so as soon as you come out of the car, you *run*. Understood?"

Poppy nodded, remembering what Peter had said: a *bird* shifter had attacked Daniel. There was no way they could possibly block birds from getting in.

Poppy wriggled out of Tristan's grip, setting her pack

down on the floor between her feet, and began digging through it. She pulled out the black scarf for her hair first, then her fleece and her raincoat. She was already wearing a sturdy pair of jeans, but she pulled out her hiking boots to switch for her sneakers.

"Yes," Tristan murmured. "Good thought."

Poppy glanced over at him and smiled, and he smiled back, holding out his hand for her pack. While she added protective clothing, Tristan drew out the three scarf-wrapped stones, her bunny and the other stuff that had been wrapped in her fleece, and the plastic bag with her phone and photos.

He tucked all of it into her shoulder bag and handed it over, saying quietly, "Under your coat, hm? Let them see the pack on your back, but not this."

Poppy nodded understanding and tucked the bag in under her loose fleece, tying it in place with the belt from her raincoat.

She'd just tucked her scarf into place when the car came to a stop; Tristan reached out to steady her with a hand on her shoulder. Sunderland and Peter were talking on radios to the police outside, throwing uneasy glances out the windows. Poppy didn't see anything, but she didn't think she'd be the first one to spot danger if it was here.

"No one's spotted anything," Peter said finally. "But we don't have our own bird shifter in the air and there's every chance they won't move until we move."

Poppy eyed the distance to the plane's open door, where a uniformed man stood waiting. It wasn't *that* far. How long could it take to run that? "I'm ready. Let's just do this."

Tristan squeezed her shoulder. "I'll be with you."

She looked him over—his bare face and hands and throat—and opened her mouth to say that he should have more protection, they should be more careful.

Tristan shook his head the tiniest bit and leaned in to give her a quick kiss—not last, it couldn't be their *last* kiss.

Then he opened the door, jumping out and pulling Poppy after him, and she was running with his hand on her arm, dimly aware of other people also pouring out of other vehicles all around them.

She kept her head down, her eyes on nothing but the ground she had to cover, and when her foot hit the metal stairway up to the plane's door, she thought, *Almost there, practically there.*

And then she tripped—no, Tristan *shoved* her—and she heard a furious raptor-shriek from above her. She tried to flatten herself on the stairs as she heard the beating of wings, too close, and then...

Something roared, and she heard other wings, and before she could think at all Tristan was hauling her up to her feet and there were other hands as well, all but carrying her the rest of the way to the plane. They didn't let go once she was inside, hustling her away from the door, and Poppy scrambled out of their grip to get to a window.

There was a bright red *dragon* out there, holding a struggling hawk in its claws. As Poppy watched, the dragon landed and police rushed in to secure the hawk; the dragon shifted back into human form—it was *Peter,* Peter had shifted and saved them.

And then a blur of black knocked Peter to the ground, and too many bodies piled on to see what happened to him.

She heard Tristan hiss through his teeth, and realized he was peering through the window beside her.

"What—Tristan—"

"That was Nikolai, I think. Hard to tell one black wolf from another at this distance, without much scent to help."

Poppy looked back—people were still struggling, and Peter was on the bottom of that pileup. "What—is Peter, Tristan, is he going to—"

"He's tough, the police are with him, he'll be all right," Tristan said, but he didn't look away for another few seconds. When he did, his face was immediately creased with worry. "Oh, no—my own, I'm so sorry."

Poppy shook her head. "What, no—"

"No," Tristan said, turning his head. "Bertil! First aid kit."

Then he pushed back the scarf covering her hair and said, "You're bleeding, Poppy, I'm so sorry, I didn't see. I should have covered your head better."

Poppy shook her head and a wave of dizziness hit. Tristan's hands were there, steadying her, pressing gently against a spot on her forehead. "Oh... oh that... stings?"

"Here, sit." Tristan guided her to sit on something a lot softer than an airplane seat ought to be, his hand behind her head guiding her to tip it back.

"I'm gonna just..." Poppy said, struggling to form the words and not sure at all which language she was speaking. "Just... close my eyes for a second. Don't worry, though."

~~*

She never passed out, exactly. Poppy was aware of Tristan laying a blanket over her and holding her in place with an arm across her body when the plane took off. She heard him talking on the phone—heard the tinny voice on the other end—but couldn't quite make herself understand anything more than the serious tones.

She was pretty sure they were speaking Valtyran, which was probably going to beat even the French she'd picked up as a preschooler when a family from Côte d'Ivoire lived in their co-op for the fastest she'd ever learned a language.

Getting help from a tiger spirit trapped in a carving probably meant that particular record was going to be marked with an asterisk, though. Still, it was going to come in handy, since it was looking like she would be in Valtyra for a long time now.

That would be strange, she thought, having one place to be her home—her home and Signy's too. Family staying in one place together, imagine that.

Poppy snuggled against Tristan's shoulder, thinking of that ocean vista photo Signy had sent her. *Valtyra*. Being a Guardian of the Stones, whatever that was, would mean something there; she would be someone who mattered there, someone with responsibilities, maybe. And whatever Tristan did as a not-especially-secret agent, it didn't seem to take him out of the country much. So he had a good job, evidently, and he and Poppy would be regular people there, surrounded by other people who changed shapes and heard magic stones. They would both belong.

Still, it was hard to imagine settling down and staying in one place. Tristan had to be better at it than she was; he'd grown up in Valtyra, in just one place. Maybe he would take her home to meet his family, and she would fit in among them and understand what it meant to be a part of something, to fit somewhere.

Shortly after Tristan put his phone away, the plane started its descent—wherever Valtyra was, it wasn't far at all from London, unless Poppy had lost more time than she thought she had. Near Denmark, presumably.

Poppy frowned, trying to think of where, in or near Denmark, you would hide a whole extra secret country of shapeshifting people. And mountains. Denmark didn't have any mountains that Poppy remembered, although it did have islands...

"Where are we?" Poppy asked, when the plane was on the ground and they were taxiing.

Tristan gave her a really worried look and reached out to gently touch her head. "We're... we're home, in my country. Valtyra. Do you remember—"

Poppy squeezed her eyes shut and rubbed them. The growl of the plane's engines was making it hard to hear, or to concentrate, and she was starting to get a headache, though it didn't seem to center at the cut on her forehead. "No, I know that, I meant... where is Valtyra actually located? I don't think I've ever seen it on a map."

"Oh! No, it's generally omitted. It's an island in the North Sea."

Poppy nodded, looking around. The view out the windows mostly looked like... airport, though a fairly small one. The usual empty land, for safety, seemed to give way pretty quickly to fields, at least on this side. When they made a turn, she caught a glimpse of a city.

None of it looked quite right, somehow. None of it looked like what she was looking for.

The plane was nearly motionless now, but the growl was getting louder. Poppy looked down at herself. Tristan had taken her raincoat off her at some point, but she was still wearing her fleece.

The bag was still under it, against her chest, holding the stones. And her bunny, but she didn't think her bunny was the culprit here.

"Tristan," she said, trying to keep her voice level the way he usually did. "I think the tiger is awake. And it wants to go home."

Tristan's eyes went wide, his lips parting—she would have thought something of him showing what he was thinking so easily, if she had room to think of anything but the tiger, and the words behind the growl, still not quite intelligible. The sense of them seemed clearer with every beat of her heart: *home, home, home.*

"Do you know where?" Poppy asked.

She thought she could find it if she had to—if she had to walk, the tiger would guide her. But this would be a lot faster if she didn't have to stop and listen to its directions.

And she wasn't sure she wanted to spend that much time listening to what it was saying.

"Yeah," Tristan said, bursting into motion all at once. "Yeah, I'll get a car, we'll go. I know the way."

Poppy closed her eyes and trusted him to handle it.

~~*

Poppy rode in the passenger seat of the SUV while Tristan drove, the wrapped stones cradled in her lap. She had put everything else back in her pack, but she couldn't let go of the stones. She didn't dare unwrap them, but they seemed... calmer, being held close to her.

She tried to watch the scenery, tried to listen to the occasional questions Tristan asked her, but she couldn't think. And then they came around a curve at the top of a slope, and instead of forest and fields and small towns, she was looking out at the sun shining on the sea.

The growl of the tiger seemed to settle into something like a purr, and the pounding of *home, home, home* in her head seemed to become less a demand and more like recognition.

"Are we close?"

Tristan looked over her, and she could see every bit of his relief on his face, a painfully obvious expression.

"Yeah, we're just starting up the mountain. Their mountain."

Poppy breathed a sigh of relief and sat up straighter as Tristan returned his attention to the mountain road, which was now climbing a steep grade. She could look down and see the green margin of land between them and the ocean, but most of the view was water.

They climbed higher and higher in a series of switchbacks; after two or three of those their speed dropped as the paved road gave way to dirt. A couple of miles further the road just ended, a low stone wall ringing the end of the road.

"This is where we park," Tristan explained. "We're on foot from here."

Poppy could see some tire tracks in the dust, though there were no other cars parked in the little area. She couldn't remember seeing another car on the road in the last few miles, either.

Poppy just nodded. She could feel the tiger getting excited again, eager to cover the last distance home, but it didn't seem quite so impatient.

Soon, she silently promised. *We're almost there.*

They got out of the car, and Tristan stripped off his suit coat and his shoes and socks. He opened his suitcase and packed some of its contents into a makeshift pack improvised from another button-down shirt, slinging it over one shoulder while Poppy made a sling of a scarf to keep the stones held against her chest like a baby, so she'd have her hands free for the trail.

It was a narrow, grassy track, obviously not much used, but someone had kept it clear of trees and low branches, and there were light-colored stones lining the outside edge whenever they came near a drop-off.

At one of those, Tristan hesitated, looking out, not at the sea, but the next mountain to the north. Poppy curled one arm around the stones to shush them and took his hand with the other, looking in the same direction and wondering what he saw.

Tristan moved behind her and held his other arm over her shoulder, guiding her eye as he pointed. "There. You see the red roofs?"

Poppy squinted and nodded, staring at the speckle of color in the gray-and-white height. The little town looked incredibly isolated, far distant from any other buildings.

"That's where I grew up. I don't mean to ever see it again from closer than this." Tristan said simply. "Neither of us would be welcome."

Poppy turned under his arm, looking up at him. Tristan kept squinting across the distance to his former home, then finally looked down at her.

His expression softened, and he kissed her gently.

"I love you," he said quietly. "You are my world now. And even if you were not—even if I had never found you, if I had no mate in all the world or a very different one— you must believe, I still would have hated everything my family ever tried to teach me about how shifters must keep apart from humans."

"Oh." Poppy reached up, running her fingers over his cheek. "*That* kind of small town, huh?"

She'd never been the odd one out for being *human* before, but she'd traveled enough to be visibly a stranger in other ways—and she knew Tristan would have stood out sharply in plenty of places where she had lived.

"Yes," Tristan said simply. "So I left, and I don't mean to go back. I'm sorry I don't have a big happy family to offer you, but..."

"I've got a little happy family," Poppy put in. "My mom and dad are great, and so's Signy, and—we'll build our own, that's all."

Tristan nodded, and they turned away from the view together and kept climbing, hand in hand.

She was reminded, though, to ask. "Do you know—is Peter okay?"

Tristan nodded. "Nikolai—they confirmed it was Nikolai—got a few bites in, but Peter's going to be all right, and they successfully arrested Nikolai and that hawk shifter. And Magnus approved officially seconding Peter to the investigation over there, so he'll be pleased about that."

Poppy nodded and squeezed Tristan's hand, unsure how to tell Tristan that she thought he had done the right thing for Peter when she knew so little about everything that had happened. They walked in silence after that.

Poppy was just starting to be aware of the altitude thinning the air when the path turned inward from the edge of the mountain, flattening out as it led through a narrow cleft. Tristan pushed her to go ahead of him, and she kept her grip on his hand as they walked single file, stone walls close around them, for a dozen yards or so.

The sky was still bright above them, and Poppy could feel the tiger leaning forward somehow. But she felt something else, from the rock walls or the path itself. It was welcoming somehow, as though they were already in the front hall of a house where their own bed awaited

133

them.

It's not just where the stones belong. We're coming home too, she thought, and half-ran the last few yards, with Tristan jogging along behind her, to where the path opened out again.

Poppy stopped and stared at the sight before her. The mountainside continued to rise to her left, but the wall of rock curved away as if someone had scooped out a piece to make this sheltered, green valley high on the mountain. Water streamed down the higher rock in a few places, tumbling into streams that fed a lake, and dotted around the lake were small stone buildings, slate-roofed, with tended trees and flowers around them.

Five of the cottages were closed up tight, windows shuttered, with an air of emptiness around them—Poppy was reminded of the bear stone, correct in its physical form, but lifeless. But two, next door to each other on the far side of the lake, were obviously occupied. Their front doors were brightly painted—one green, one blue—and they had thriving garden patches nearby.

As Poppy watched, the blue door opened, and the distant figure of a white-haired woman waved to them, then beckoned in a gesture clear even from the other side of the lake.

Poppy looked back at Tristan, who squeezed her hand and smiled encouragingly. Tristan stepped up beside her, and they started along the path together. It curved around between the natural wall of the mountain and the cottages, with footbridges over the streams that ran down to the lake.

Closer up, Poppy could see that something was not quite right here. Some of the slate tiles were missing from the roof of the nearest house, and cracks showed in the stone walls. The first footbridge, too, was suspiciously new-looking, as though it had recently had to be rebuilt. And some of the trees showed scars where branches had been torn away—the bright inside of the trees still showed through, not much weathered, as though it had happened this summer.

"Are there many storms, up here?" Poppy asked, looking around.

"No," Tristan said, sounding a bit grim. "We are on the lee side of the mountain. Strong storms shouldn't reach this place."

Poppy looked down at the tiger, which seemed to have gone silent, though it ought to have been ever more eager to get all the way home.

It wasn't until they were crossing one of the bridges that Poppy noticed another narrow crack in the stone wall, right beside one of the waterfalls. The crevice was shadowed, but Poppy could see stone steps rising up between the sheer stone walls, climbing higher still up the mountain.

Into its heart, Poppy thought, and curled her arm tightly around the stones she carried on her chest.

"Poppy?"

Poppy looked back at Tristan and found that he was still standing on the path, just past the bridge, but she had taken two steps off it, toward that hidden stair.

"Do we need to go now?" Tristan asked her. "Or can we go and speak to the lady of this place, first?"

Poppy looked toward the stair again. It was where she would need to take the stones, of course, and Tristan had known it without her even having to say.

But the stones themselves were still silent, and once Poppy wasn't staring at that path, she could think again.

"No," Poppy said, tearing her gaze away to look toward the cottages and the lake again, and the vista of sky and sea beyond the lip of the valley. "No, we should speak to her first. These sorts of things always end badly if you start by being rude to an old lady, don't they?"

Tristan squeezed her hand, tugging her back onto the path and curling his arm firmly around her. "That's the way I've always heard it, yes."

135

They walked along a little further down the path, and when Poppy stopped again, Tristan stopped with her. They stood at the spot where a faint impression in the grass showed that there had once been a well-worn track up to one of the cottages.

Two gnarled apple trees grew at the near corners of the little stone house, and its door, though faded, had been painted red. It seemed in good repair, its roof intact and the walls solid. More than that, Poppy thought it looked particularly welcoming, somehow.

"Yes," Tristan agreed, though she hadn't said anything, only stood and looked. He kissed the top of her head, and added, "But not quite yet, my own."

Poppy nodded and thought again, *We're coming home.*

Then she turned with Tristan and continued down the path to the woman who awaited them at its end.

13

TRISTAN

Tristan hadn't seen the village where he grew up in years; as a guardsman he hadn't often had reason to venture up into the mountains, and the Captain of the Guard, Magnus, had spared him the difficulty of going back to the place where he was born. Men of the Royal Guard set aside all their old connections, but there was no reason to test that unnecessarily.

He had expected to feel a sense of loss, looking across the distance between mountains to that place, but mostly what he had felt was Poppy at his side, tucked under his arm. He had felt certain that the past was in the past, and he could leave it behind.

And then they had entered the Home of the Guardians, and he had felt as though he had stepped into his home village again—without all the burden of his father's unyielding expectations, the rigid adherence to rules he had never agreed with or entirely understood.

This was a different home, welcoming and kind, and though he had never seen it before he felt as if he had always known it, as though his feet knew the path already. He understood the stair as soon as Poppy took that dreamy-eyed step toward it, and he knew that the house with the apple trees would be his home as soon as he saw it.

His and Poppy's, and, perhaps soon, the family that they would make.

But there was no ignoring the quiet of the place, the signs of damage and the emptiness all around them. What should have been a small but bustling village stood almost entirely deserted. There were no children here.

The path curved around to the house with the blue door, and the woman who had waved to them was waiting on the grass beside it, with an equally aged man at her side. Both of them were dressed sensibly in sturdy trousers and soft shirts, hiking boots on their feet. They stood together in such a way that it was clear, without them touching or looking at each other, that they were mates, and had been for longer than Tristan had been alive. They were two halves of one whole together.

"Welcome," the woman called out. "Come closer, my dear, let me see—" Then she stopped short, her hand going to her heart.

Her mate quickly wrapped his arm around her, supporting her as her ruddy cheeks went pale.

Poppy slipped out from under Tristan's arm and hurried to her, and Tristan stayed right at her side. There was no danger here, he knew, but there was an urgency. Even though Poppy was no longer lost in the strange delirium that had gripped her until they reached the mountain, he knew it still pulled at her—and that it pulled at this guardian as well.

Poppy dropped to her knees in the dust of the path, and the woman—the Senior Guardian, surely—knelt as well, with her mate's arm supporting her all the way down. Then Poppy drew out the wrapped bundles she had carried like they were her own children, and the woman gasped, tears springing to her eyes.

"Oh, the tiger and lion, both! Two of our cats are come home together—" The woman stopped short as Poppy hesitantly drew out the third stone. The bear, the one she had treated so casually.

"I... I don't know about this one," Poppy said. "I thought... maybe it's just that I can't hear it, or..."

The woman took the little wrapped shape from Poppy with shaking hands, unwrapping it to reveal the white bear. She let out a rough breath, and her mate dropped to his knees beside her as she raised the stone to her lips, kissing the top of the bear's head, right between its ears.

"The bear stone." Myrthild nodded sad confirmation. "When the stones were betrayed, the bear stone was not only taken away from us into exile. It was... unmade, most cruelly. I was its special guardian, left alive to long for it, and you have brought it home in time. Oh, my dear, you are not too late."

She leaned in to hug Poppy, who, with her hands occupied by the stones, could only lean into the embrace, tucking her head down onto the woman's shoulder while the woman and her mate each wrapped an arm around Poppy.

"Thank you, thank you," the woman whispered. "Thank you, my dear. You have brought them home. It has been so quiet here for so long, and I began to think that we would crumble down to the sea before we could bring back any life at all. But I have lived to see this."

Poppy drew back, her eyes darting from the house with the blue door to the one beside it. "Are there no other guardians left? Only you?"

"Only I, of the guardians who were here before the stones were betrayed. My name is Myrthild, and this is my mate, Fredrik. My granddaughter, Estella, lives in the next house. I think in the proper way of things she would have been my successor as the bear's guardian—well. Now perhaps she yet will be. Perhaps it will help her to know there is hope."

"I'll go and tell her," Fredrik said, pressing a quick kiss to his mate's cheek before he stood. Myrthild stood with him, the bear stone tucked against her heart, and Tristan helped Poppy to her feet as well.

"Come, come and sit comfortably, not in the dust of the road. You must have come a long way, my dear. Tell me your name?"

"Poppy Zlotsky," she said. "I was born in America, but... I came the long way around, this year. The tiger seems to have taught me Valtyran overnight. And," she glanced up at Tristan as they walked over to a worn wooden bench set in the sunniest spot by Myrthild's cottage. "This is my mate, Tristan."

Tristan couldn't help beaming at Poppy when she said that, and Myrthild laughed as she sat down. "Newly mated, then?"

"Very," Tristan said. "Not... quite formally, in fact."

"Mm," Myrthild said, frowning slightly. "Well, as long as you're sure of each other, that's bound to sort itself out."

Tristan nodded to himself at that. He *could* be sure of it; he had the king's decree in his suitcase, declaring his release from the Royal Guard effective as soon as he set foot in Valtyra. He had belonged only to Poppy for, oh, nearly an hour now.

Tristan looked to Myrthild, meaning to ask her whether it mattered, especially, that a guardian and her mate had formalized their bond. But she was looking past him, and her shoulders sagged with some disappointment. Tristan looked over his shoulder and saw Fredrik returning alone.

"Estella has not been well," Myrthild explained. "But with two of the stones returned... I had hoped the sight of them might help her, but I think nothing will be better until they are truly back where they belong."

Poppy stiffened beside him, her grip on the stones tightening, and then she twisted to look back toward that narrow stair up into the mountain. He could feel that tension in her body again, the pull of her duty to the stones. For a moment, when they reached this valley, it had seemed that she was finished, or as good as, but it was obvious that there was more to do.

"Ma'am," Tristan said. "Should we go now?"

Myrthild gave a sad smile as Fredrik came around to stand behind her. "I think that will be best, much as I wish I could offer you proper hospitality first. I can feel the... the gap, between where they are and where they ought to be, and I expect Estella can feel it, and Poppy..."

"I feel it," Poppy said quietly. Her eyes were fixed on that crack in the stone. "I don't know why they're being so quiet now, but I need to take them the rest of the way home."

She looked up at him then, and her expression turned almost pleading. "Tristan, will you come with me? I don't want to try this one without backup."

Tristan smiled, wide and automatic, cupping one hand to her cheek, his heart soaring at the knowledge that she *asked*, that she wanted him there even for this most secret and sacred of tasks.

"Of course, my own. I'll go anywhere with you, you need not ask."

Fredrik cleared his throat rather ominously, drawing Tristan's attention. "No man is a Guardian," Fredrik said firmly. "And no man may walk the Guardian's path."

Tristan felt his tiger growling at that. He wouldn't let Poppy go alone again. He couldn't.

"Tristan," she said softly, leaning into his grip, though he could still feel the way the stones tried to pull her away. "Please. I have to do this, and clearly, the sooner the better. You're the one who told me I was meant for this. You know I can do it, don't you?"

Tristan closed his eyes and turned, hugging Poppy close with the stones between them. "You can do anything, my own. But I hate not being there to help."

141

"Walk me over there," Poppy said softly. "I won't leave you until I have to. But I have to do this, so I can come back to you."

Tristan nodded against her hair. He shrugged his makeshift pack off, and helped Poppy shed her big pack without having to let go of the stones cradled against her chest.

"Is there anything I should know?" She looked over at Myrthild, who still held the bear stone and showed no sign of giving it up soon. Clearly, if the bear was going to be returned to the mountain, Myrthild would carry it. "Anything I should do, or not do?"

Tristan began searching the pockets of her pack, pulling out a flashlight, a multi-tool, a small length of parachute cord. He tucked the useful items into her pockets as Myrthild spoke.

"You'll know, I think. I... don't know exactly what it will be like, to tell the truth. I have not ventured in there in many years, and I do not know how the heart of the mountain will react to the one who brings the stones home. It has been unsettled, and unhappy, since they were taken."

"Unsettled?" But before Poppy had even finished the word, the mountain itself seemed to answer: the ground underneath them shifted and then shook. Tristan caught hold of Poppy, dropping to his knees before he could fall and curling himself protectively around her.

He couldn't let her come to harm again today, not while he was still with her, not when there was anything at all he could to do help.

A rising howl came from the second cottage, and a woman in a nightdress, her hair dark and wild, ran out and fell to the ground. She spread her arms wide and pressed her face to the earth, wailing like a siren all the time.

The earth shook and shook, and Tristan looked up warily at the rock face that curled around the little valley. Small rocks tumbled down here and there, but there was no loud crack or roar to warn of a coming avalanche. Not yet.

As soon as the shaking stopped, he jumped up, and Poppy moved with him. Without further speech, they both ran toward the crack in the rock while Fredrik and Myrthild ran to Estella, still wailing even though the earth was now still.

Tristan was afraid that the narrow passage would be blocked, but he could see, when he came even with it, that it remained clear.

For now. If the earth should shake again—if Poppy should encounter something in the heart of the mountain that tried to prevent her, some test or obstacle—she was a guardian, but not a Valtyran. She was human—strong for her size, capable and smart, but breakable and so slim and small in his arms. He held her for a last second, kissed her forehead beside the bandage and then kissed her lips one more time.

"I have to," she whispered.

"I know," he replied. "Go with my love, my own."

Poppy kissed him again, and then she turned and charged up the ancient carved steps, disappearing into gloom as Tristan watched. He stepped closer, trying to keep his eyes on her for as long as he could without offending whatever spirits might shake the earth while she was inside.

When she was entirely out of sight, his gaze dropped to the steps, and he noticed something. The steps were old, worn down by the passage of feet over the centuries, but here and there he could see claw marks scraped into the stone.

He looked back over his shoulder. Myrthild was kneeling, cradling Estella in her arms, but Fredrik was on his feet, watching.

The old man—the mate of the Senior Guardian—nodded to him, and Tristan was sure. He didn't bother stripping out of his clothes, just kicked off his shoes and shifted, letting the tatters fall away as he settled into his tiger shape.

No *man* could walk the Guardian's path. But the guardian's mate was not only a man. He had lived for so long hiding his true face, his true form, controlling himself and behaving more human than humans—but Poppy had taught him to let go, to show himself to her, and he knew she would not fear him.

Tristan raced up the stairs, claws digging into the stone, ears tilted forward to listen for any sign of his mate, any warning rumbling of the stone around him. All was quiet. So far.

14

POPPY

Poppy charged straight up the stairs, not letting herself think beyond what she had to do. She didn't dare look back at Tristan or she would be trying to find some way to bring him along; it hurt to be separated from him, and she...

She really didn't want to have to figure things out all alone, once again. That was what it was supposed to mean that they were mates, wasn't it? She was supposed to have him with her, on her side.

The stairs entered a tunnel mouth, and the dimness of the shaded stairs became real darkness. Poppy closed her eyes in gratitude for Tristan and pulled her small flashlight out of her pocket. She shone it around and discovered five openings from where she stood.

She reached into the makeshift sling and unwrapped the stones, knowing that she needed to listen to their presences now. They knew where they belonged—they had brought her this far.

What she heard, when she waited there in silence, was a soft padding of feet behind her. She turned just as a tiger—*Tristan*—bounded into view.

Poppy grinned, understanding immediately. "You are no man, ha! Oh, Tristan, thank you, I'm so glad—"

She wrapped her arms around his enormous furry neck, only having to bend her knees to do it. She heard a huge low rumble, like a diesel engine trying to purr, and one enormous paw touched lightly on her hip.

Poppy?

She jerked back at the sound of Tristan's voice, looking at him. She heard him, and yet he clearly wasn't speaking in any ordinary way. "Tristan?"

Yes. I wasn't sure if this would work, but if you can hear me, I might be able to help beyond just... He bared his teeth in demonstration of what he would most easily be able to help with, in this shape.

"Thank you," Poppy whispered, hugging him again, and then she turned to look at the five tunnels again. This time, with her tiger beside her and the tiger and lion stones against her chest, it seemed obvious which way she needed to go.

Poppy strode confidently toward the second opening from the right.

As soon as she stepped into that tunnel, her flashlight flickered and went out. Poppy froze, feeling an instant of unreasoning terror in the darkness. She clicked the button for the flashlight a few times, but nothing happened.

Shh. Close your eyes and be still, Tristan told her. *Put the flashlight back in your pocket. Don't you know cats can see in the dark?*

"Ha," Poppy said, but she shoved the flashlight into her pocket, setting her hand on Tristan's furry shoulder instead. His warmth and the solid weight of him beside her were a comfort, even if not quite the way she would have imagined if he could stand beside her and hold her hand.

When she opened her eyes, she still couldn't see anything at all. Her hand tightened on Tristan, her heart beating faster.

Shh. I can see. It's level here. Come with me. Trust me. Keep your eyes closed.

Poppy closed her eyes again, for the illusion that there would be anything she could see if she only opened her eyes. She kept a firm grip on Tristan and moved with him, one step at a time. She didn't know how long she walked beside her mate in the darkness, trusting him to guide her, but after a time he stopped.

Poppy?

Poppy risked opening her eyes. The darkness was still absolute. "What is it?"

Her voice didn't echo, but seemed to be strangely swallowed up by the weight of stone around them. There was no sound at all but their breathing, Tristan's louder than her own. She knelt and leaned against his broad, warm side to feel his breathing, her hand still clinging to the fur over his shoulder.

I can't see now either, he admitted after a moment.

She could feel his frustration at being unable to simply solve the problem for her, and she pressed her forehead against his ribs, thankful that he was still there with her, even when the darkness was too great for either of them.

"There has to be a way," Poppy said, making herself think it through.

Myrthild had said she would know. What did she know? What did any guardian know?

She knew how to listen to the stones.

Poppy forced herself to let go of Tristan, still leaning against him, as she quickly unwrapped the two stones she held against her chest, setting down first the lion and then the tiger on the ground before her.

Tristan still stood completely motionless, still deaf to the presences in the stones. Poppy knew that she had to let go of him to really hear them, but in the darkness she felt as if she might never find Tristan again if she lost contact with him now.

"I have to listen to them," Poppy said, her voice

147

shaking, her cheek pressed against Tristan's fur to hear his great tiger heart beating. "I have to—I have to let you go."

I won't leave you, Tristan promised. *I'll be right here. I won't ever leave you alone.*

He didn't make it easy for her and take a step away. He stood there, letting her lean against him for as long as she needed to before she gathered herself and moved, knee-walking one sideways step away from him.

The presence of the lion and tiger were suddenly all she could sense, so vivid she could smell them, hear them, almost see them even in that utter darkness. She could sense their wildness, their power. If these spirits had ever shared a soul with a human shape, it had been a long, long time ago. She had no idea how to ask them for help, how to be guided by them.

"Tristan? Do you know what the stones are *for*? They're not just—ancestors, or gods, are they?"

No, Tristan said. *They're our source. The king, together with the Guardians, can use them to make humans into shifters. I don't know how it works—the Guardians have always been set apart on their mountain, and the stones were stolen before I was born.*

The guardians used the stones to create new shifters. Meaning they could, what, siphon off a little of this wild, ancient tiger spirit and put it into someone? Place just enough tiger inside them to make them a shifter, without draining all the spirit from the stone, without overwhelming a human with a tiger they couldn't control.

"All guardians are human, aren't they," Poppy said. "Guardians have to be human."

Yes, Tristan said. *When I was young I was told it was the reason that humans were sometimes born in shifter families. So there could be guardians.*

There wouldn't be room in a shifter for another piece of the tiger in the stone. Only a human, a guardian, could bring part of the tiger out of the stone, and pass it on—that part must be where the king came into it.

But Poppy didn't need to give the tiger in the stone to

anyone. She only needed to bring it far enough out of the stone to talk to her.

"Okay," Poppy said. "I'm not sure what's going to happen here, but I think I know what I have to do."

I'll be here, was all Tristan said. *I'll do anything I can to help.*

"Can you pick up the lion stone and take it a little way away?" Poppy tapped her fingernails lightly against the lion stone, feeling the lion just on the other side of that surface—but not nearly as interested in her as the tiger was, and not really hers to be so close to, she knew.

Tristan moved, following the small ticking sound, and she felt the hot gust of his breath before his teeth closed gently around the stone, picking it up like the tiniest kitten. He carried it away until Poppy could feel nothing but cool, empty space around her.

She kept her eyes squeezed shut and hurriedly unlaced her hiking boots, skinning out of her clothes, just in case this worked the way she thought it might.

Poppy? What...

"Just a hunch," she said, and then she knelt on the cold stone, and closed both of her hands on the tiger stone.

Please, come here, show me the way to bring you home.

She heard a growl, felt an impossible leap across no distance at all, and then felt the tiger within her, bright and strong and too big for her skin to contain. She felt herself stretching all over, changing, her smooth skin to striped fur, her arms and legs thickening, her fingernails turning to wicked claws.

Poppy looked around as the tiger and found she could see everything. Tristan, standing a little distance off, was watching her intently, holding the lion stone in his mouth still.

He was, she now realized, quite a well-made tiger. She had only been able to see *Wow! Tiger!* before this, but now she understood what a tiger should be, and preened with the realization that her mate was quite an excellent one.

Poppy?

Yes, she said, reminded that her mate was waiting for her to finish what they had come here to do. She carefully picked up the tiger stone between her powerful new jaws, carrying it as delicately as she would a kit.

This way, she told Tristan. *We're almost there.*

Then she leaped forward and began to run, enjoying the power of the tiger's form. Her mate was right on her heels, unhesitating as he chased her, and she led him through one twisting tunnel after another, never setting a foot wrong. There was a place where they had to leap over an abyss that seemed bottomless, dark even to the tiger eyes the stone had given her, but she cleared it easily, and an instant later Tristan landed right behind her.

What was that? He asked. *Why did we jump it?*

Poppy stopped, nearly tumbling over herself with the momentum she'd built up. *Couldn't you see?*

No, I told you I couldn't. I'm following you.

Stay with me, then, she told him, and ran onward into the mountain's heart.

15

TRISTAN

As soon as he saw a glimmer of light ahead, Tristan pulled even with Poppy. He had smelled and heard the change in her, sensed it, but to see her at his side as a tigress was something else entirely. They matched this way, fit together in a way he could never have imagined fitting with Poppy. For all that he loved her human, it was wonderful to share this with her, to have her really know what it was to be a shifter, a tiger, at his side.

He had only a moment to feel that before they reached the tunnel's top, emerging into the dazzlingly bright day near the top of the mountain. Just outside the tunnel the ground was unnaturally flat, smoothed into a sort of plaza. A blackened hearth at the center was cold and empty, and around the circle of the plaza was a low wall.

There were nine obvious niches in the wall, and a number of smaller ones arranged around and between them.

The great stones and the small, Tristan recalled, from some old story. The great stones are for the oldest, largest clans—there was only one bird stone, the raptor. But different bird clans made their own stones and placed them here. The same for other kinds of shifters.

The tiger and lion are both great stones. The lion—there, where the gold of the sun will reach him.

Tristan nodded and carried the stone to the spot Poppy had indicated, thinking of Kai, their new crown prince, soon to be king. What would it mean for his clan, his line, to have the stone returned to its place?

Tristan set down the stone gently in its niche and turned to watch Poppy place the tiger stone a little way around the circle. Tristan would have smiled, in his human form, at Poppy's obvious instinct not to put the great cats too near each other.

There must be balance, Poppy told him, backing away from the niche, her tiger tail flicking a little. We can't be all cats for too long—the lion and tiger will fight for ascendancy, and all other clans will suffer.

Poppy shook herself all over, stepping close to the tiger stone and nosing at it. Tristan moved a little closer, not wanting to interrupt her obvious focus. He could sense that there was something unfinished here, the ritual not yet completed. He glanced at the cold hearth again, then back to Poppy, who was focused wholly on the tiger stone.

She tore her attention away from it suddenly, looking at him with wide eyes, uncanny green in her tiger's face. Tristan. How do I change back? How do I put the tiger back?

Tristan hurried to her then, pressing close to his mate as he began to feel her struggle to shift. She hadn't really done it herself, the first time; she had let the tiger spirit from the stone enter into her, and it had shaped her into this tiger form. But she wasn't—hadn't been—a shifter, and had no real control over it.

Remember who you are, Tristan told her. Remember what you are. You are human, my own.

But I am not.

ROYAL GUARD TIGER

It was not Poppy's voice, and Tristan jerked back from the vastness of it, coiling himself as he snarled. Poppy's eyes glowed an unearthly gold, the shape of her changing further, growing large. The tiger spirit was taking over.

Leave her. Tristan snarled aloud. She is your Guardian, not your vessel. She carried you home, she has done what you needed.

What would you know of what I need, cub? I have been locked in that stone, alone, for countless years.

Tristan roared and lunged at the uncanny tiger. He kept his claws in, his teeth far from her fur, but he had a feeling that touching Poppy—his Poppy, however hidden in the shape of the tiger—would help her find her way.

Leave her!

He bowled the tiger over, and suddenly the form under him was not a tiger but his own Poppy, slim and human, fragile and small and pale under his paws. She was horribly still, her bright eyes closed, and he barely had time to catch the sound of her heart beating before he heard another tiger's roar and moved to stand between her and the tiger spirit—now separate from her, looking solid though Tristan had a feeling it could not be, or not for long.

You belong in the stone, Tristan insisted. You will be honored again as you always should have been. You are home now.

The tiger snarled and Tristan leaped at the same time it did, meeting it in midair to keep it away from Poppy lying limp on the stones.

I could have a home in her, the spirit offered, even as Tristan snarled and grappled with the all-too-solid thing, his claws turned aside by thick fur, his teeth unable to get a grip. I could leave a part of myself in her always. She would be a true match for you then, a shifter like you. You could take her home.

Tristan roared right in its face, flipping the tiger spirit onto its back with a furious heave. She is my mate, just as she is. I would not change her against her will to please

153

anyone. Now release her and return to where you belong.

He heard Poppy stir behind him and roared again, bracing himself to keep the tiger spirit pinned down—but as suddenly as it had appeared it vanished. Tristan spun around to see Poppy kneeling by the stone again, pressing one pale hand against its surface.

Tristan shifted human himself, hoping she hadn't seen too much of that—she was the special guardian of the tiger stone, she might not like him fighting its spirit that way—but when she turned away from the stone she threw herself into his arms.

"Thank you," she gasped. "For a second there it was— it was like I wasn't there at all, it was just swallowing me up, and then—"

"You were right, that's all." Tristan held her tight against him. "Sometimes you need backup."

Poppy nodded, her red hair flying wildly and shining like copper in the sun, and Tristan pulled her up higher in his arms to kiss her. She kissed back just as eagerly, fiercely, pulling back only to say, "Plus I got to see you fight tiger style, that was—"

Tristan kissed her again, harder, torn between shame at her having seen him that way and an undeniable urge to claim his mate, now that he had won her from such a powerful adversary. They were both naked, and Poppy's skin felt hot and soft against his; he was hardening for her with every beat of his racing heart, and he needed her. He needed her to be his, entirely, only.

"Yes," Poppy gasped, "yes, Tristan, please."

Tristan pulled back just enough to see that beyond the little plaza at the tunnel's mouth, there was a grassy slope. He carried Poppy to the low wall surrounding the stone plaza and let her down on the other side. He bounded after her in the next second, but Poppy was already running away with a laugh, following a curve of the slope up higher.

Tristan followed her, tackling her gently to the turf in a

spot with a dazzling view of the ocean. He caught her hands and pressed his mouth to the nape of her neck, and Poppy went still under him, suddenly pliant.

"My own," he whispered. "My Guardian to guard, now and forever."

"Yes." Poppy wriggled deliciously under him, pressing back against his hardness so he could feel her, soft and sweet and yielding under him. "My sweet tiger, make me yours, make me—"

Tristan slid one hand under her then, cupping and teasing her breast as he kissed the back of her neck, nipping and sucking to make pink marks that showed brightly on her pale skin. Poppy rippled and writhed under him, pressing her hips back against him as she wordlessly begged for more.

Tristan slid his hand down then, over the little curve of her belly and between her legs. The curls there were already wet, and when his fingertips found her secret folds, she was wetter still, and hotter.

Poppy was moaning, rocking her hips between his hand and his cock, as if she didn't know which she wanted more. Tristan moved over her, nudging her thighs apart and angling her hips up. Poppy's hands closed into fists, tearing up the green grass and sending that sweet smell into the air, making the tail end of summer smell like the start of spring.

He lined himself up and slid inside her, his way slicked with her desire, and though he meant to be gentle he couldn't stop from pushing to his full length in one fast slide. Poppy cried out, but she was pushing back against him as she did it, joy and pleasure evident in every line of her body and humming intangibly between them.

My mate. Tristan kept moving inside her, wringing sounds of bliss from her as he struggled to control himself when her body wrapped around him so sweetly. After a little while he moved, kneeling up and bringing Poppy with him so that she was sitting on his lap with him buried deep inside her.

"Oh, oh," Poppy gasped at the change in position, throwing her head back against his shoulder and moaning with pleasure.

Tristan had both hands free to touch her, then, stroking at the little bud between her legs with one hand, making her writhe in ecstasy, rising and falling on him as she did. His other hand explored her, stroking her breasts and all her lovely fair skin as it flushed pink with exertion and delight. He bent his head to nibble at the side of her throat, and she twisted to kiss him.

She was breathing too hard to keep her lips pressed to his, but Tristan kissed her again and again as he made love to her, driving her to the brink of pleasure. It wasn't long before she went over it, her body tightening around him as she cried out against his mouth.

Tristan held her to him, thrusting into her a last few times before he found his own release, spilling deep inside her as he held her. He buried his face against her shoulder as he caught his breath, still gripping her tight.

He felt Poppy's heartbeat slowing, her breathing steadying from its pleasured frenzy, and his own body was soothed by hers. After a time he picked his head up and looked out with her from their great height. They could have been the only people in the world up here on the mountaintop, looking out at the sparkling ocean.

Finally they eased apart, walking quietly back down the grassy slope to the plaza. Tristan stopped short at the sight of a small, blue flame lit in the hearth at the center.

"Ha," Poppy said, squeezing his hand and looking up at him with a bright-eyed smirk. "I thought it might be something like that. I bet at least one of us can see the way back down in the tunnel, too."

Tristan shook his head and caught her up for another kiss before they headed back down the mountain, hand in hand.

16

POPPY

Poppy picked up her clothes in the tunnel when they reached them. Tristan was still in his tiger shape, just in case the tunnel wouldn't allow him to pass the other way in his human shape, and Poppy was still flying too high on the success of her first act of guardianship—and lighting that fire with Tristan—so she didn't bother putting them back on until they got down to the bottom. She had assumed Tristan's clothes would be waiting there, all neatly folded, but instead discovered a bunch of tatters of cloth piled together with Tristan's shoes and socks. Someone had, tactfully, left a folded blanket.

Poppy covered her mouth but couldn't quite stifle a giggle, even as her heart went warm with the awareness of how Tristan had rushed to join her as soon as he realized how.

Tristan himself just gave a tiger's chuff and shifted back to his human shape, and Poppy found that in bright sunlight, at least, she could detect a flush on the tops of his cheeks and ears. She kissed him again when she had her clothes on and he was wearing the blanket like a cape, somehow managing to look dignified while carrying his shoes and what was left of his clothes.

They didn't go far down the road before they spotted their packs beside the door of the house with the apple trees.

"Go on in!" Someone shouted, and Poppy turned to see Fredrik standing at the curve in the road. He waved to them happily. "It might be a bit dusty, but it's all yours!"

"How is Estella?" Poppy called back, and even at a distance she could see Fredrik's wide smile.

"Much better! Thank you, Guardian!"

Fredrik turned away, leaving them to explore their new home. Poppy had barely pushed the door open before Tristan was crowding up behind her, lifting her into his arms. The blanket slipped rather precariously, but they were nearly inside.

Nearly, but not quite. Poppy beamed up at her mate as she realized what he meant to do, looping her arms around his neck and tugging him down for a kiss before he stepped inside, carrying her over the threshold and into the home they would share.

It was dim inside, making it hard at first to tell anything about the house at all. The windows were all covered with wooden shutters that let in only slivers of light. Poppy wriggled out of Tristan's grip after one more kiss, eager to explore, and went from one room to another, throwing the shutters wide.

The windows had no glass in them, and there certainly was plenty of dust. Poppy thought the fine layer had been shaken loose by the earthquake more than accumulated in its years of absence.

But the little house stood solid and sturdy, and the wooden furniture was old-fashioned and beautiful, and had weathered the years of neglect, as well as the recent shaking.

The house was nothing grand—not like the hotel room

she'd stayed in with Tristan—but it was cozy and bright, once the windows were open and letting in the mountain air and sun. There were two slant-ceilinged bedrooms upstairs. One would be their bedroom, Poppy instantly decided; there was a big bedframe there already, though without a mattress. She looked at Tristan across the width of it, and the heat in his eyes kindled an answering warmth in her, though she could still feel the delicious ache from earlier between her legs.

Tristan glanced down at the bedframe, and the bare wooden floor beneath it, and said, "I'm going to... look around downstairs."

Poppy grinned at his retreating back and didn't argue; nothing in the house was even as soft as the grass up on the mountain's peak. They couldn't just make love outdoors here in the valley, with Myrthild and Fredrik and Estella only a few doors down, so they would just have to find a way to furnish the house more comfortably as soon as they could.

Poppy listened with half an ear for the sounds of Tristan looking around downstairs as she went across the landing to the other upstairs bedroom. It was small, and entirely unfurnished, but... just right for a crib, she thought. There would be room for a rocking chair, too, by the window with a view of the sea.

She lowered one hand to her belly. She knew it couldn't be happening yet—the little bump of a birth control implant was still there in her upper arm, assuring her that she and Tristan wouldn't be surprised until they were ready to be. Still, she could imagine rocking a baby, their baby, here. Making a family here, where they would have a home that stayed put, waiting for them.

She thought back to when she had arrived in London, thinking that it would take her weeks of thought to decide what to do next. She thought of that restless searching feeling that had pushed her onward for as long as she could remember, and she realized it was now still.

It wasn't just the relief of the need to bring the stones home—she had found what she was looking for here. She didn't know whether that was Tristan, or the stones, or this place, this home, or the idea of the future they could have.

She thought maybe she had always been looking for all of that and now, all at once, she'd found it.

"Ha! Found it," she heard Tristan call from down below, sounding further away than just one flight of stairs.

Poppy turned away from the window and hurried down to find him—a little round-topped door in the kitchen stood open on another set of stairs leading down. These steps were stone, but a light glowed down below, and Poppy followed them down into something between a cellar and a basement. There were no windows, but the floor was paved cleanly in stone, and the walls were lined with shelves that held wooden boxes and chests of all shapes and sizes.

Tristan was kneeling over a wide, low chest, painted red with little decorations of blue and green and white. He was reaching down under what looked like a layer of blankets and sheets, prodding at something. He looked up at her and gave her a wide-open smile.

"Mattress," he said succinctly. "Wool-stuffed, probably. It's been folded up and tied down to keep it in the chest, so it will need some fluffing to get it back into shape. We should take the whole chest upstairs before we take it out."

Poppy looked around again and realized that all the house's furnishings must be here, things put away after the last guardian had left, packed carefully to protect from earthquakes or time.

"Glass for the windows," Tristan said, pointing to a stack of wide, flat boxes under the stairs. "If we get those in place it will be a bit quieter."

Meaning, Poppy realized, her face going hot, their new neighbors wouldn't hear them breaking in the bed.

"Right," Poppy said, going over to grab one handle of

the trunk with the bedding. "Looks like we've got some moving in to do."

Tristan laughed, but he closed the lid and helped her carry it up the stairs.

~~*

They had set up their bed and installed the first two of the glass windows when Myrthild came up the path with a basket.

"Supper, and a few other supplies," she said, as they came to meet her. Tristan took the basket from her hands, and Myrthild smiled and took a step back. "I won't keep you, I know how it is—new-mated and making your first den together."

Poppy grinned and thanked her, but she saw a certain shadow in Myrthild's eyes as she turned away, and her steps were hurried.

Poppy suspected that she didn't want to be away from Estella too long, and that "much better" than however unwell Estella had been before was not quite the same as "entirely recovered."

When she looked at Tristan again, he was staring into the basket as if it held the secrets of the universe. "Tristan?"

He looked up, and his expression had gone unreadable, making her realize how open and happy he'd looked since they came down from the mountaintop together.

"What is it?"

He nodded, as if to say, *Yes, there is something*, but he said only, "Let's go sit by the lake and eat."

The late afternoon shadows were beginning to stretch longer, but they were both warm from their work, so it was pleasant to sit down at the edge of the little mountain lake. They pulled out bread and cheese and sausage, fruit and salad and little cakes from the basket, and for a while they ate in silence, Tristan staring out at the lake while

161

Poppy mostly watched Tristan.

She was a little startled when he looked back at her, but she smiled and he smiled back before dropping his gaze. "I think I dreamed about this place, after the first time we made love. Of being here with you, and our... our future."

Poppy was almost certain *future* wasn't the word he'd meant to say there.

"Was that... magic, do you think? Have you ever been here before?" She looked around at the quiet and added, "Are other people allowed to come here?"

"Allowed, yes, at least this far. Few have bothered, since the stones were lost, and even before then, not many, I don't think. I hadn't, ever." He looked out at the lake again and shook his head. "That's... you told me to think of whether there were more things I hadn't told you, and I was trying to think of the things I haven't told you. That's... not the most important one. But it's the one I like the best."

Poppy stood up and moved around to his other side, so the detritus of their picnic wasn't between them. She snuggled up to his side, and Tristan's arm came around her, warm and steady, reminding her of the night they met. "Tell me some more?"

Tristan sighed. "I told you your sister sent me to find you, and that Otto had tried to... remove her."

Poppy nodded, starting to see what he was getting at.

"The reason she could send me and the reason she was conspired against..." Tristan tugged her half into his lap, curling his arms around her but getting enough distance that they could look each other in the eyes. "Did you know that your mother was married once, before she met your father?"

Poppy nodded. "To Signy's dad, you mean? You don't have to tell me she's my..." *Half-sister*, Poppy didn't say, as she realized that Signy's father must have been Valtyran, a shapeshifter.

Tristan nodded. "Her grandfather summoned her to

Valtyra—sent me to America along with Kai, and Otto, to find her. Otto was First Minister, you see, and Kai and I were guardsmen. And Signy's grandfather is the King of Valtyra."

Poppy's jaw dropped. For a stupid, jealous second, all she could think was, *Oh, of course, I might be a Guardian of the Stones but Signy's a princess.*

Then she saw the scars on Tristan's face and throat—really saw them for what they were, not just part of Tristan's face but the evidence of violence and betrayal.

She touched her fingers to his cheek. "Otto... didn't want an American princess?"

Tristan tilted his head. "He didn't want a princess who knew her own mind, and her own mate. Signy is human, just like you are, so it is her husband who will rule Valtyra—Otto meant to choose for her, but Signy and Kai knew they were mates as soon as they met. They are Crown Prince and Crown Princess now, and soon they will be married. And... it may not be long, after that, before they become King and Queen."

Poppy leaned against Tristan's chest, hiding her face for a moment.

"But you are a Guardian," Tristan said softly. "And the Wisdom Stones are the heart of Valtyra, as my mate is my heart. And we shall have our own future here, because you had the courage to find the stones and bring them home."

Poppy nodded, twisting to look out at the lake again. There was plenty of room in Valtyra for her and for Signy, after all. And she wouldn't have wanted to be a queen, but Signy would probably be pretty good at it.

"Do you have anything else to tell me?" Poppy asked after a while.

Tristan nuzzled against her hair and said, "Sometimes you snore and it's adorable."

Poppy burst out laughing, elbowing him a little, and Tristan fell back to the grass as though she'd really knocked him down. Poppy could have followed him down, tickled him or kissed him or done something else to keep them rolling in the grass as the sun sank on the other side of the mountain's peak. Instead, she took a breath and said, "Do you have a phone that gets service here? I need to call my sister."

~~*

Poppy went inside and started a fire in their fireplace, perching on the hearth while Tristan got back to putting the glass windows in. He was near enough to watch, and near enough to hear at least her side of the conversation, but not hovering.

The phone rang for a while, and just when Poppy was wondering what to say in a voice mail and thinking that it had been stupid to imagine a *Crown Princess* would be free to answer her phone whenever Poppy called, Signy picked up.

"Tristan? Is Poppy okay?"

Poppy covered her mouth with one hand at the sound of her sister's worried voice, struggling for a second to compose herself before she said, "Hi, Siggy. I'm fine."

"*Poppy!*" Signy's shriek was halfway between delighted and exasperated, and so familiar that tears came to Poppy's eyes. She looked up to see Tristan watching her, and he winked and returned his attention to the windows when their eyes met.

"Pops, I'm so glad you called, because I was trying to give you time but I was also honestly going to call out the rest of the Royal Guard to track you down if I didn't hear from you soon. But you're all right?"

"I'm fine," Poppy repeated. "I'm, uh, I'm a Guardian of the Stones, as it turns out? Apparently that's... important."

"*You're—*" Signy's voice altered, clearly aimed at someone else. "Laila, could you just get Kai? *Immediately?* Tell him I require *a word* about tomorrow's schedule."

"Siggy?"

"It's fine, it's fine, I'm just going to strangle Kai before I even get around to marrying him," Signy said. "I was losing my mind wondering where you were and whether I was going to find out before we had to head off to some mountain first thing tomorrow morning because there's an urgent ritual that he and my grandfather have to do with some special stones, and no one thought to tell me that the heroic young woman who brought them back to Valtyra today is *my sister Poppy*."

"It was going to be a surprise!" The masculine voice must belong to Kai, her soon-to-be brother-in-law.

"Oh, a surprise like *my sister Siggy* being a *princess*?" Poppy asked.

Signy was silent for a moment. "Um..."

Closer to the phone, Kai said, "I like you, Poppy. Welcome to the family."

Poppy giggled. "I'm reserving judgment, Kai. But it does sound like you're well on your way to treating my sister like a queen."

Signy finally started laughing, and Poppy was laughing nearly too hard to hold the phone; Tristan came over after a while and she leaned against him while he got all the details from Kai about when they would be arriving the next day (very early) and what preparation was required (none, except to be prepared to get up very early).

Poppy and Signy managed a few apologies and *see you tomorrow*s before Tristan hung up the phone and tugged her to her feet. "Come on, we need to get the rest of these windows in before it's time for bed. And our bedtime is very early tonight."

"And at some point we'll have to go to sleep, too," Poppy agreed.

~~*

Myrthild and Fredrik joined them the next morning to

greet the little party who had come up the mountain. Poppy had wondered if there would be a whole entourage, but it was just Signy and her gorgeous blond mate Kai, the white-haired king, and another man with a similar big build, who was soon introduced as Magnus, the Captain of the Royal Guard.

He was older than Tristan, but there were only a few glints of silver in his dark brown hair. The trip up the mountain clearly hadn't troubled him, unlike the king, who was still catching his breath.

"Magnus was my boss, until yesterday," Tristan explained in an undertone, while the king and Myrthild and Fredrik were explaining to Signy exactly how they were related to each other—Myrthild was some kind of cousin many-times-removed to Signy, and Estella was therefore a different kind of cousin.

Poppy looked up at him and a flash of guilt went across Tristan's face. "Should I have remembered to tell you that I had to quit my job to stay here with you?"

Poppy squinted at him, then said, "I'll let it go, I suppose."

Tristan stole a quick kiss, just before everyone's attention turned toward them, Myrthild saying, "And you know of Poppy of course—she brought home the lion and tiger stones, though I haven't yet had the story of just how she came to find them. She is the tiger's special guardian."

The king stepped forward, holding out both his hands. Poppy was pretty sure you weren't supposed to *hug* kings, but it also didn't seem like she was supposed to curtsey—no one was exactly standing on ceremony, in this deserted village at six in the morning. She tried holding out her own hand, the one Tristan wasn't keeping a grip on.

To her surprise, the king clasped it in both of his and kissed it. "Thank you, Miss Zlotsky. You have done us a greater service than you can possibly know. Any Guardian would be honored throughout the kingdom, but you have done more. You have brought our heart home to us."

"...Oh," Poppy said, looking up at Tristan and over to Signy with her eyes wide, not sure what to do. "You're... welcome?"

The king simply squeezed her hand and released it, still smiling. "Well. We shall express it properly another time. For now—Kai, Magnus, Fredrik, Tristan, come with me to speak to the stones. Ladies, if you will excuse us."

Poppy nodded, and Tristan hugged her tight one more time before he followed the king with the other men, and then Signy caught her in a hug.

"You *will* come to the wedding, right?" Signy asked, when she let Poppy go a little.

Poppy nodded helplessly, and Signy said, "Good. Because Laila's figured out about six options for your dress, and I need to know what you think. And get your measurements."

Poppy's eyes went wide, wondering what she was getting herself into.

Myrthild laughed. "Come, come back to my home, girls. We'll have tea, and I know where to find my tape measure."

167

EPILOGUE

Tristan looked at Poppy, ten days after they met, and smiled down at her as they went to their audience with the king.

Today was the day of the royal wedding, but the earliest parts of the ceremony—conducted at dawn, and mostly private—were already over. Everyone had changed into their finery for the main ceremony. Tristan wore a tuxedo rather than a guardsman's dress uniform for the first time, and Poppy looked radiant in a silk gown of some rich blue-green shade that made her eyes look as bright as the sea.

She beamed up at him now, almost skipping as they walked through the palace. She was already wearing a gold tiara set with sapphires, loaned from her sister for the occasion, but her neck and shoulders were bare.

There was no mystery, and no need to worry, about why they were being called before the king today.

It was the same audience chamber in which Tristan had been given his mission to find Poppy and bring her to Valtyra, though the company was somewhat expanded. Kai and Signy were both present, as well as Poppy's parents, but also Magnus and the King's Council—such as it was, these days, having lost four of its members after

169

Otto's treason came to light.

Signy—Crown Princess Signy, in her full formal role, which she had settled into as if she'd had rather more than a few weeks' practice—made introductions all around. Poppy was new to the councilors, of course, and Tristan was nearly as unknown. As a guardsman he had been virtually invisible to these men despite seeing all of them in and around the palace for the last ten years.

Soon they assembled themselves properly for their real purpose. Poppy took her place before the king with Tristan standing at her shoulder, while Kai and Signy flanked the king. The Zlotskys and the councilors were to either side, witnessing.

"For your great and courageous service to the Kingdom of Valtyra," the king said, "I award to you, Poppy Zlotsky, the Royal Order of the Bear. All your life you shall be, in your own right, *Lady* Poppy of Valtyra."

Poppy knelt to receive the marks of her honors, smoothly rearranging her skirts as she had practiced while Magnus stepped up with the velvet pillow on which the items of her regalia were arranged. The king first bestowed the yellow sash of the order with the white and gold star-shaped badge. After that came a heavy gold chain that hung over her shoulders, a plaque with an enameled white bear resting at the center of her chest, just above the neckline of her gown.

There had been much practicing when they came down to Bjornholm from the mountain last night, to be sure Poppy knew how to wear everything. Which was to say nothing of the frantic communication to be sure that the neckline of her dress would be precisely engineered to accommodate both the sash and the chain.

Poppy arose, back straight and chin up, and took her step back to stand beside Tristan. He beamed at her, and she was grinning radiantly at him, blushing a little as all in the room applauded her, including the king—and her sister.

Tristan looked around and found that one person wasn't looking at Poppy—Kai was looking at Tristan, grinning widely, and he mouthed, *Wow.*

Kai had never seen him smile like this, but Tristan had a feeling that his friend was going to have plenty of time to get used to it; it seemed to happen so easily when his mate was by his side. Tristan grinned wider, helplessly, and returned his attention to Poppy.

"Now," the king said. "There is one other matter which I wanted to bring before you all—Lady Poppy, this concerns you as well, so I have not used your honors only as a pretext."

Poppy's expression turned serious, and she held Tristan's arm tighter as she looked up at him, a question in her eyes.

Tristan gave a tiny headshake. He had had no idea of the king having anything further to say either.

"My reign is drawing to a close," the king said simply, in such decided tones that none could make even a token protest that he might rule for years yet.

"The past few years, this recent treachery, though defeated, has made the need for it clear. Such a thing would not have happened when the Wisdom Stones were all in place at the heart of Valtyra. And while Valtyra shall be all the better for having two stones home, they require the balance of another—the bear stone must be remade."

Tristan looked at Kai, who was staring steadily forward. Obviously *he* had been briefed on this already, as had Magnus, who was equally controlled. The councilors stirred uneasily.

"Remaking the stone requires gifting it with a bear spirit—I do not pretend that the one I possess is the equal of that which was taken when the stones were stolen, but I shall give all that I have, and hope it is enough to revive the stone. I am assured that I shall survive the process, but..."

The king looked over at Signy with a wry smile. "I shall

be entirely human afterward. I shall therefore step down from the throne—retire—some months from now, in the spring. This will allow time to make a smooth transition to the reign of our next king and queen—who shall choose their own Council."

Magnus looked down at that, and Tristan realized that, though he was not technically a member of the King's Council, it would likely mean a great change for him, as well. Kai had known Magnus as his commander, and Magnus had known Kai as a guardsman—could they be king and captain to each other? Would Magnus retire as well?

"We shall have many meetings to discuss all this entails," the king added. "And a formal, public announcement will be made before too much longer, so that the people of Valtyra will also know what is to come, and who will lead them. But all of you in this room deserved to know first."

"Now." He clapped his hands together. "Today is a day of celebration, and we still have a wedding to attend! Let us not keep our Prince and Princess waiting too much longer."

Everyone smiled at that, and the formality of the moment broke up as they all headed out of the small audience chamber to find their places for the wedding. As they walked back out into the midday sun, Poppy's new regalia glinted in the light.

She looked down at it, running a finger along the heavy gold links, then up at Tristan. "I still think you ought to have gotten something too. I couldn't have done it without you."

"I was only doing my job," Tristan replied, keeping a firm grip on his mate. "And besides, I already have all the reward I could want."

THE END

ABOUT THE AUTHOR

Zoe Chant loves writing paranormal romance! Over a hot cup of tea (or something stronger), she whips up sexy tales of hunky heroes and adventurous heroines to tantalize and satisfy her readers. Sizzling hot romance, no cliffhangers!

Join Zoe's mailing list to receive email notifications about her new releases:
http://eepurl.com/bhOy_T

17615324R00105

Printed in Poland
by Amazon Fulfillment
Poland Sp. z o.o., Wrocław